UNDERTONES OF WAR . . .
AND OVERTONES OF MURDER

"I'm ever so sorry to trouble you, Doctor, but it's the foreman from the building site. They want you to go across there straightaway."

He got to his feet. "An accident?"

It looked like an accident to William as he left his own house and started across Conway Street. All the men who had been working there were all standing round the bottom of the site in a little crowd.

"This way, Doc," one of them shouted, spotting him.

Another held a ladder while he climbed down to their level. He supposed they were in what had been the cellars of the bombed houses. He picked his way across to the waiting group.

They were looking down at a body.

A LATE PHOENIX

by Catherine Aird

BANTAM BOOKS
TORONTO · NEW YORK · LONDON · SYDNEY

*All of the characters in this book are fictitious,
and any resemblance to actual persons, living or
dead, is purely coincidental.*

This low-priced Bantam Book
has been completely reset in a type face
designed for easy reading, and was printed
from new plates. It contains the complete
text of the original hard-cover edition.
NOT ONE WORD HAS BEEN OMITTED.

A LATE PHOENIX
*A Bantam Book / published by arrangement with
Doubleday & Co., Inc.*

PRINTING HISTORY
*Doubleday edition published January 1971
Serialized in Seventeen Magazine, November 1971
Bantam edition / April 1981*

ISBN: 0-553-14517-7

Published simultaneously in the United States and Canada

For Philippa Buckley
with love

Brief quotations at the start of each chapter are taken from Mrs Beeton's *Cookery and Household Management.*

*Burial in private ground is permissible
unless such use of the ground amounts to
a nuisance . . .*

1

Dr. William Latimer gave the screw a final twist. It was the last of six screws. Four would have done the job quite well but he was a careful, cautious, and conscientious man and he had used six.

Carefulness, cautiousness, and conscientiousness were the three good "c's" which had been drilled into him at his medical school by the lecturer on medical ethics. Then the same lecturer had gone on to warn the class against the other three "c's." The bad ones. Those which led a doctor into danger—conduct, canvassing, and covering.

Conduct (infamous in a professional respect) didn't trouble William. If any lady patient had designs on his spotless professional reputation there was always the redoubtable Miss Tyrell within earshot. Miss Tyrell was his receptionist and secretary. Ramrod thin, austerely dressed and bleak of expression, she could be guaranteed to quell any patient with a look. Miss Tyrell stood no nonsense from anyone.

Canvassing was another unlikely risk. He had come to this practice precisely because it was small. That had been what he had wanted. Somewhere not too ambitious where he could make a good beginning in general practice without very much outlay.

Covering meant he mustn't set up in practice with a faith healer or lend his backing to any other medically unqualified person. Dr. William Latimer had no intention of doing this. He was on his own in his practice and he intended staying on his own.

1

After the last twist of the screw he stepped back and took another look at the plate on the wall.

W. LATIMER, M.B.,CH.B.

He had paid attention at those lectures; more, perhaps, than the rest of the class because he didn't come from a medical background or even a professional one. Doctors' sons, he knew, learnt these matters at their fathers' knee. They came strangely to him, the son of a carpenter.

He twisted his lips wryly. He was what was known as first generation pinstripe. He picked up the measure, the spirit level and the screwdriver—there were some things he *had* learnt at his father's knee—and wondered how soon he would be able to afford to have the house painted.

Before very long, he hoped. There was no denying the general air of neglect about Field House. His predecessor had let things go and then he had died and there had been more neglect while the National Health Service Executive Council had sorted out the practice and his executors had wound up his estate.

William Latimer's gaze shifted upwards a fraction and rested on the plate above his own.

HENRY TARDE, M.R.C.P., M.B.,CH.B.

It was brass and was polished daily though Henry Tarde had been in his grave nearly two months now. That was nothing, though, compared with the third plate on the wall. That had been rubbed to illegibility, though if you stood very close and knew what you were looking for you could still make out the name MANDERSON.

Field House had been a doctor's surgery for a very long time. True to a medical tradition that he *had* heard about, William Latimer had left both plates on the wall above his own. It was a sort of professional ancestor-worship, he supposed, because if anyone wanted to consult Dr. Manderson now they were something like thirty-five years too late.

2

Standing as he was, so close to the front door of the house, he found himself really looking at it for the first time. In its way it was quite a fine piece of work, though there was no doubt whatsoever that it needed painting. A bit of putty wouldn't come amiss either in some of the cracks. There was an architrave which his father would have approved of, though the left-hand abacus was badly split.

William glanced over his shoulder.

That would have been the bombing. Doctors' houses were like public ones and often stood at a street corner. Field House was no exception. It, too, was on a junction of four roads. And the opposite corner was still a bomb site.

Now he came to think of it, that was one of the things which contributed to the general air of neglect that he was so aware of. He had been told that the St. Luke's area of Berebury had caught the worst of the town's bombing in the last war. Certainly there were still quite a few tattered bits of ground dotted among the otherwise tightly packed houses.

Once, though, it must have been a very well-to-do part of the town because Field House was a substantial building—late Georgian, early Victorian, decided William. And it had been built in a field—hence the name.

William felt he should have looked at the deed of Field House and made sure about its date but he had really only had it in his hands for a matter of moments. That had been in the solicitor's office, when they had been en route between Henry Tarde's bank and his own Building Society. And, he thought ruefully, at this rate it didn't seem likely that he was going to see them again for another thirty years or so.

At least the bells on the doorjamb didn't look as if anything needed doing to them. And he could vouch already for the fact that they worked. The day one, anyway. So far no one had tested the night bell beside it. That was another thing that was only a matter of time. He knew that. Sooner or later he was going to be dragged from his nice warm bed in the middle of the night to somebody else's bedside. He hoped it would be

3

later if only because he didn't know the streets of his practice in daylight yet—let alone in darkness.

Underneath both bells was another circle of polished brass. Instead of a push-button inside it, though, there was a plug on the end of a little chain. This was the most old-fashioned method of all of summoning the doctor from his bed. It was a speaking tube which led—William Latimer knew not by what devious route—to a spot in his bedroom wall just level with his pillow.

A preliminary whistle from street level presumably shot him into wakefulness and then he unplugged his end and had a cosy chat with the caller. What the doctor's wife thought of this arrangement he did not know and he, William Latimer, had not yet taken unto himself a wife to ask.

He walked up the three steps to the front door and turned round. His practice—though he still thought of it as Henry Tarde's practice—was literally all about him. There were no other doctors in the St. Luke's part of town. The nearest were in Vittoria Street and they were the consultants. Vittoria Street was Berebury's own local Harley Street.

William had wanted to call it Victoria Street at first—the Old Queen having left her name on a quite remarkable number of thoroughfares—but he had been corrected by the precise Miss Tyrell. Vittoria, he was told, had been a battle in the Peninsular War at which the local regiment—the West Calleshires—had acquitted itself with distinction. Hence the street name.

There were no other doctors in St. Luke's because there was no longer any need for them. In that area of the town which lay nearest to the Market Square the shops and offices had pushed the homes and the people who lived in them farther and farther away. In the east—the poorer houses always seemed to be in the east end—the Town Council had cleared many of the tight little streets and built fine new houses on the outskirts of Berebury.

So now the roads were clogged every morning and evening with those same people coming back into the town to work, to shop, and to school. At the other end

4

of St. Luke's—the Park Street end—the prosperous folk had gone even farther out—to the villages—and they commuted to their offices and shops and professions each day too.

Yet St. Luke's wasn't a twilight zone. Berebury was too old a town for that. Some of its loveliest houses were right in the centre, and there would have been more of them too but for the bombing. Nevertheless these exoduses at each end of the St. Luke's area had meant that William Latimer had come to a small practice. Dr. Henry Tarde had been in Field House for a long time and it would seem that his practice had diminished nicely for him as he grew older and would have wanted less work.

William Latimer opened the door. Soon patients would start coming to the surgery door as they had been coming every Monday morning for the last hundred years and more. Somewhere he could smell his breakfast cooking, though—alas—the meals served by his housekeeper, Mrs. Milligan, did not always live up to their olfactory promise.

He still paused for a moment before he went indoors. It was one of those startlingly lovely September mornings, all the more enjoyable because it carried with it the unmistakable message of autumn.

There were other changes in the air, too, besides the weather. It looked as if some time soon the corner opposite Field House was going to cease being a rough tangle of broken brick and overgrown weeds. Just before eight o'clock this morning a lorryload of men had turned up and begun to spread themselves over the old bomb site.

Actually the first thing they had done had been to erect a little shelter and start a brazier going but, that achieved, they had started clearing the larger trees and erected two boards. MARK REDDLEY AND ASSOCIATES (DEVELOPERS) LTD proclaimed the first, a well-lettered and discreet advertisement. The second, altogether a more casual affair, was propped up at a drunken angle against a few bricks and said simply GARTON AND GARTON, BUILDERS, BEREBURY.

Dr. Latimer looked across at the workmen and noted

5

the immediate contrast between them and those young archeologists who had been digging the same site all weekend. William had paused yesterday morning and looked down at their carefully laid string and little trowels. There had been four men and a girl and they had scratched about all Saturday and Sunday.

He had called out "Any luck?" to them at one stage yesterday.

Their leader, a young man with a beard and wearing open sandals, who the others addressed as Colin, had shaken his head ruefully. "Nothing Saxon yet."

William Latimer wasn't an archeologist but he would have said they needed to look no further than themselves for Saxon remains. The girl with them, industriously crouched beside a narrow trench, was pure Saxon, long blond hair falling unattended over her bent shoulders.

He had seen them all troop away, tired and dispirited as the light went last night.

The arrival of the workmen explained the archeologists' concentrated work over the weekend anyway. After this morning there was obviously going to be no chance of investigating any old civilisation here. The second half of the twentieth century wanted to use the space.

He watched the workmen for a few more moments.

The odd thing about their leisurely pace was that it actually got anything done at all, but it did. Their breakfast was under way, too. The tantalising smell of sausages cooking on their open brazier drifted across Conway Street and reminded him how hungry he was. He turned on his heel and went indoors. Miss Tyrell would not expect him to be late for morning surgery.

He wasn't quite sure whether he had inherited Miss Tyrell as secretary-cum-receptionist or if she had merely inherited him as Dr. Tarde's successor. A bit of both, he decided fairly, as she greeted him after breakfast from her little office beside his consulting room. Perhaps she was like the fixtures and fittings specified in the briefly seen deed of the house.

Perhaps she just went with the practice.

"Seven new calls, Doctor, only one of them urgent. I said you'd go there first."

Geographically his was a close-knit practice and he passed his own house (well, his own and the Building Society's) several times during the course of the morning while he set about seeing the seven new calls and any number of old ones. On one occasion he was just in time to see a large yellow vehicle at work on the old bomb site.

It looked more like an artificial cockroach than anything else. With consummate ease it tugged up a well-established elm tree. Not only with ease, but without ceremony. There was no surrounding circle of watchers while somebody shouted, "Timber." Nobody shouted anything as the yellow thing went into reverse gear and simply pulled. And that in spite of the fact that the tree could have been all of twenty-five years old. Uprooted, the yellow machine dragged the tree to a corner of the site where two men with bandsaws descended on it without delay.

Miss Tyrell took a gloomy view of the noise.

"It'll go on for months, I expect, Doctor. And this is only the beginning. You wait until they start with their pile drivers or whatever it is they make their foundations with."

"Yes, indeed. No, no sugar, thank you," murmured William. Miss Tyrell had conjured up coffee to coincide with his arrival—almost as if she had been expecting him.

"Dr. Tarde always used to come back about now," she said, "to see if there were any new calls."

"Oh?" he said oddly disconcerted. "And are there?"

"Not this morning. There quite often are." Miss Tyrell consulted a list in front of her. "If you should pass this way again and see the sitting-room curtains drawn you'll know that something else has cropped up and I'd like you to come in."

"Thank you," said William gravely. At least he would know now that it didn't signify a death in the house. . . .

Miss Tyrell ran her eye round the consulting room. "Otherwise, Doctor, I think everything's all right."

"Thank you," he said again.

7

"Mrs. Milligan's gone out shopping. I'll do the letters and the filing until she comes back. And I'll be back in time for evening surgery."

"Right." He didn't want to stand in the way of Mrs. Milligan going shopping. "Tell me, Miss Tyrell, what's going to be built opposite?"

Miss Tyrell's hatchet face grew longer. "Shops of some sort, Doctor, I think, but there's been so much argument about that site over the years that I'm sure I don't really know what the upshot will be."

"Argument?"

"Plans," she said lugubriously. "First one lot and then another and then somebody wouldn't sell and then he would—only by then the Town Council wouldn't let him build what he wanted. There was talk of a compulsory purchase order at one time—or so I heard—but nothing came of it." She sniffed. "And before it was all settled they started this business about a ring road."

"Here?" he said, dismayed. "You mean just outside my house?"

His and the Building Society's, of course, but all the same . . .

"That's right," she said. "But you needn't worry. They changed their minds about that too."

"I'm very glad to hear it."

"Everyone's changed their minds so often," she said grimly, "that it's just as well there are some people left who can still get things done."

William Latimer abruptly decided it was time he got back to his round. He drained the last of his coffee. "How do I get to Shepherd Street, by the way?"

Miss Tyrell told him.

The next time he took a look at the bomb site was after his luncheon. Mrs. Milligan's visit to the shops had meant a piece of steak which would have been nice if it had been cooked properly. William took a little stroll along Conway Street preparatory to going out on his afternoon round. These were the less urgent cases, the chronic sick, and the very old.

Like a magnet the sight of other men working drew him back to the bomb site corner.

He wasn't the only one. The spectacle had also at-

tracted an elderly man who was leaning on a stick, two
small boys, and a young woman pushing a pram. There
was a baby girl in the pram who was patently delighted
with the workmen.

"Dada," she said impartially.

"Dada," she said, catching sight of William.

But it was the elderly man whom William recognised.
He lived in the house farther down Lamb Lane—next to
the bomb site—and was called Herbert Jackson. He
had chronic bronchitis, and William had already treated
him.

He waved a stick at the bomb site. "They ain't rushed
themselves, Doc, have they?"

"Well . . ." said William consideringly, looking at
the workmen, "it's heavy work, you know."

"I don't mean today, Doc," wheezed the man. "I
mean since it happened."

"Oh, haven't they?"

"The morning after this little lot copped it they was
round from the Council promising to rebuild. And such
houses as you've never seen. With everything you could
think of inside . . ."

"That wasn't yesterday," agreed William.

"Yesterday? It was in 1941, Doc. Wanted us to
move out and all." He pointed to the shored-up wall of
his house. "Only temp'rarily, mind you. Till they got
going on the building again."

"Did they?"

"Just as well we didn't go. We'd have been waiting a
tidy while afore they got round to touching this little
lot."

"That's true," observed William.

"Said my house wasn't habitable, they did . . ."

"Really?" William cast an eye towards Bert Jackson's house in Lamb Lane. It looked to him as if it was
being held together in some grotesque wooden corset.

"Not habitable," snorted Bert Jackson. "As I said to
them, if the landlord collects his rent it's fit to live in, in
spite of the Borough Engineer and all his mob." Jackson wheezed away. "And sure enough, come the Friday
he was round. And he's been round every Friday ever
since."

William murmured that landlords were like that.

Jackson waved his stick again. "Bert, boy, they said to me, just you wait until this bloomin' war's over and we'll build a proper row of houses fit for a lord, they'll be. Well, Doc," he wheezed, "I waited, but I reckon unless they look sharp I'll be dead afore they're finished."

"Nonsense," said William warmly. "You'll live to be a hundred."

The big tree had almost gone now.

The logs that had made it up were being tossed on to the contractors' lorry. The leaves and the twigs and the other surface detritus from the site were being heaped onto a bonfire. Someone had driven a surveyor's stick into the ground, and another man was knocking in little wooden crosses for sight lines.

Considering that they had only started work that morning, the men had made a fair impression on the site.

William could see quite clearly when the bomb must have fallen. The remains of the other houses told him that. On the end of the house in Conway Street which had once joined the bombed buildings was a new brick wall, less weathered than the rest of the house. The other house which abutted the damage—old Bert Jackson's house—was round the corner in Lamb Lane. It hadn't been so lucky in its repairs or, perhaps, the party wall hadn't been so badly damaged in the first place. The timbers were shoring up a torn wall. He could still see where the bedroom fireplace had been and the jagged holes climbing the wall which had meant the staircase.

Field House must have been damaged, too, decided William, swinging round on his heel and taking a good look. Once he started looking for damage he could see the patches in the roof tiles. And odd chips on the facing.

"Look at the pretty flowers," said the woman with the pram to the baby.

"Dada," said her daughter automatically.

The men had started tearing up the remaining greenery on the site. William peered down.

"Epilobium augustifolium," he thought. He had resented botany and he still resented it. Its connection with medicine smacked to him of herbalism and ancient unscientific, uncertain remedies, but it had been on the curriculum and he had had to learn it. The men were scooping up great armfuls of the plants now, scattering the seeds to the four winds.

The young woman with the pram nodded to him. "Funny how that stuff always grows on places like this, isn't it?"

"Rose bay willow herb," agreed William, mentally abandoning its Latin name. "Hardy."

"No," said the young woman. "That's fireweed, that is."

He got back from his afternoon round just before five o'clock, looking forward to a quiet cup of tea before evening surgery at six. He had barely sat down when Mrs. Milligan came in, wiping her hands on her apron.

"I'm ever so sorry to trouble you, Doctor, but it's the foreman from the building site. They want you to go across there straightaway."

He got to his feet. "An accident?"

It wouldn't be surprising with all that machinery about—or had Bert Jackson fallen into a hole?

Mrs. Milligan frowned. "I don't think so, Doctor. He just said he'd be obliged if you'd step over there as soon as you could."

It looked like an accident to William as he left his own house and started across Conway Street. It had all the earmarks of one. All the men who had been working there were standing round the bottom of the site in a little crowd. They were staring but doing nothing— just like they did when someone had been knocked down.

"This way, Doc," one of them shouted, spotting him.

Another held a ladder while he climbed down to their level. He supposed they were in what had been the cellars of the bombed houses. He picked his way across to the waiting group.

They were looking down at a body.

11

2

It wasn't so much a body as part of the remains of one.

A skull.

"It was Mick here what found him, Doctor."

One of the labourers was pushed unwillingly to the forefront of the small crowd.

"Sure and I didn't know he was there at all." Mick was small and wiry and Irish. "Just swung my pick, I did, wi'd'out tinking." He peered anxiously at William. "I didn't do the poor fellow no harm, Doctor, did I?"

William shook his head. This body was well beyond all harm.

"I swung my pick and there he was," insisted Mick, "lying there."

That was quite true anyway. Though only the skull and the cervical spine had been exposed by the blow from Mick's pick-axe the skeleton gave every appearance of lying flat in the ground face upwards.

"Some poor bloke what caught it in the bombing, I expect." One of the younger labourers, not born then, looked round the torn site wonderingly.

The foreman, a compactly built man with more self-assurance than the others, said, "Let's hope so, Patrick, me lad, else you'll be short of a bit of overtime come the end of this week."

"Me, Mr. Burrows?"

"All of you," said the foreman grimly. He turned to William. "Unless we can get this shifted tonight, Doctor?"

William shook his head. "It's not for me to say, but I wouldn't count on it."

"If it's a question of help with the digging, Doctor, I'm sure we can . . ."

"It's not," said William briefly, going down on his knees and taking a closer look at the skull. "I'm not an expert, Mr. Burrows—I'm only a general practitioner, you know, but I'd say that he or she . . ."

"Strewth," said one of the men standing by. "Not a bird. . . ."

There was indeed something utterly unfeminine about the skeleton.

"You mean that could be a she, Doctor?"

This was obviously something they had none of them considered.

"Could be," said William noncommittally. He didn't know a great deal about skeletons. Moreover, what he did know was based on a highly polished, fully articulated model called Fred that had accompanied him through his medical student days and which, truth to tell, bore very little resemblance to this dirtbound decaying shape.

"Well, I never . . ."

Immediately they all crowded round again and took another look.

William noted with wry amusement that they appeared less uncomfortable in the presence of a skeleton than they would have been with a dead body.

By now someone would inevitably have covered a dead body. That was an instinct too deep for words: a feeling he had heard someone say that came with the dawn of civilisation, marking its very beginnings—consciousness in man.

And the next stage, they said, had been when man did not marry his sister. Now, who had that been? One of the medical school professors, he supposed. That was the trouble with lectures. You didn't know which bits were the ones that were going to be important until it was too late. . . .

"It's been here a goodish while," said William, still professionally cautious. "I wouldn't like to say it wasn't the bombing. . . ."

"That's something to be thankful for anyway, Doctor." Burrows, the site foreman, looked quite relieved.

14

"Why?"

"I was afraid it might be historical," said the foreman, "and then we'd be properly in the cart."

"Oh? Why's that?" William was now squinting down at the skeleton's teeth. It still had practically a full set.

"A real mess we'd be in then, and no mistake," said Burrows savagely. "I've had that happen to me on a site before now, Doctor, and believe you me, I've had cause to regret it." He pointed down at the skull. "And it wasn't even a body before. Do you know what it was?"

"No . . ." murmured William absently. Those teeth had a meaning, he thought, if he had a minute in which to work it out. "No, I don't."

"A vase."

"A vase?"

"That's right. A perishing vase." The man Burrows grimaced. "And we couldn't do a ruddy thing about it except grin and bear it."

Kneeling down beside the skull William thought he could detect a grin there, too. There was something macabre about those teeth. . . .

Burrows was still fulminating about the vase.

"Nicest piece since the Portland the old dodderers kept on saying." He shrugged. "But it didn't look anything special to me."

"No?"

'They tell me it's in the Greatorex Museum now," said Burrows, "not that that was any consolation at the time, I can tell you."

"Quite," said William.

"Before you could say 'knife'," went on the foreman, in whom the injustice of the vase had obviously bitten deep, "the place was swarming with people and we lost the best part of a fortnight's work—good work, too. That wasn't all, either, Doctor. . . ."

"No?" William had grasped the significance of the teeth now. Surely a full set like this must mean someone relatively young. . . .

"No," said the foreman seriously. "There was a penalty-clause in the contract and the firm caught a cold."

15

"Oh, dear." William wasn't really paying attention to the man.

Burrows waved an arm. "And I don't mean your sort of cold either, Doctor. The site owner said he didn't know this old vase was there and the developer said he didn't see why he should stand the racket and as for my firm. . . ."

"Yes?"

"My firm said it wasn't their fault the thing had turned up . . ."

"No, of course not."

"Though I suppose you could say," said Burrows heavily, "you could say in a manner of speaking it was." Here Burrows glared at the luckless Mick. "Anyway, they lost."

"Did they?"

"They'd contracted to finish by a deadline and they hadn't." He sucked his lips expressively. "Not a penny bonus for anyone on that job."

His audience clearly didn't like the sound of this. A big burly fellow standing next to the man called Patrick stirred. . . .

"It's all right, Jack," said Burrows promptly. "The union didn't want to find any vases but there wasn't anything they could do about it either. Not once it had been found."

Jack subsided, nodding.

William Latimer looked from one face to another. In the main they were young men—though the big chap called Jack was older; and they wore cheerful, dirty clothes under their virulent red-coloured monkey jackets. Not a single man had string tied round his trouser legs in the old labouring tradition. Any more than Mr. Burrows had a bowler hat to distinguish him as foreman.

He didn't.

His authority was based on something different but it was there all right and they all listened to what he had to say.

"It was the lawyers," insisted Burrows. "They argued that these archeological remains hadn't been provided for in the contract. And it wasn't what the contract meant that counted. It was what it said. You know what lawyers are."

William nodded. They were about as well understood by the lay public as doctors.

"They'd got everything else you could think of in." The foreman wrinkled his brow. "Strikes, lockouts, civil commotion, Acts of God, force majoor—the lot."

"But not vases," said William sympathetically.

"Not vases." Burrows indicated the skeleton. He grinned. "They have now. Archeological finds are the responsibility of the site owner."

"That means we'll be all right then after all, Mr. Burrows, does it?" asked a lanky man anxiously. "I got mouths to feed at home."

William Latimer coughed. "I'm afraid I can't swear that this is—er—archeological, you know."

All eyes turned back to William.

"It's too well preserved for one thing to be all that old and the little bones are still here." That was one of the things he did remember from his anatomy lessons. The smaller bones disintegrated and disappeared first. If they were still present it meant something. "I'm sorry, chaps, but I can't certify that these are Saxon remains or anything like that. They could be—er— quite young, relatively speaking. I'm afraid that means the police and the coroner."

Mr. Burrows groaned aloud.

Mick, the Irishman, was beginning all over again. This time his voice had a distinct keening tone to it. "Just swung my pick, I did, wi'd'out tinking. Making a daecent hole for the marker, I was. The digger's got to come tis way first ting in the morning and . . ."

"Not now, he hasn't, Mick."

There was a small silence while this fact sunk in.

"It'd go right through where he's lying, mate."

Mick looked at the skull and let his glance travel along the ground.

"If the rest of him's under there," said Burrows ominously, "where we think it is . . ."

The skull, noted William, was still obstinately male.

" . . . then the digger would have had him."

Mick's mate, Patrick, did an expressive scoop with

17

his big hands. "And then we might never have known he was here. Man, that digger really digs. A couple of goes and the driver not really looking and that would have been the end of him."

"On the other hand," remarked the observant Dr. Latimer, "they very nearly found him yesterday from the looks of it."

"Yesterday?" said Burrows at once.

"The archeologists. Look where they were digging . . ."

"Pretty near," agreed the foreman. He looked down at the archeologists' neat little trench in very much the same way as the captain of an ocean liner might have regarded a cabin cruiser. "Thank goodness they didn't find him or we'd never have got on to the site at all."

William moved over the rough ground a little. "It looks to me as if it was a nearer thing than you might think, Mr. Burrows. Look over here. You can see where they drove their first markers in and then changed their minds."

"Wonder what made them do that?" said Burrows politely, but he obviously wasn't really interested in the vagaries of the archeologists. What he was interested in was the present and the immediate future. He stepped back to the crowd. "Would one of you lads go and find a copper, smartish, while I try to ring the firm? Mr. Garton'll want to know about the holdup as soon as possible . . ."

William finally straightened up. "There's just one other thing, Mr. Burrows. If you've found this body and it did happen to have been the bombing . . . "

"Yes, Doctor?" Burrows already had his foot on the bottom rung of the ladder.

" . . . then there may be others here too."

"Oh, no there won't," said the foreman flatly. "I've told them not to find any more."

The Consultant Pathologist to the Berebury and District Hospital Group Management Committee was Dr. Dabbe.

It was slightly more than dusk by the time he and Detective Inspector C. D. Sloan got to the site. Sloan

18

was the head of Berebury's tiny Criminal Investigation Department. It was so tiny a department that if there were any odd jobs going it got them too. This was one of the odd jobs.

In spite of the dusk they were not short of light. The contractors had rigged up arc lamps so that their own men could go on working after dark.

But not tonight.

Dr. Dabbe and the police were the only people working on the site tonight.

"It's human, Sloan," said the pathologist immediately he saw the skull. "At least they haven't got us out here for an old sheep."

"No, Doctor." Sloan wouldn't have minded particularly if they had. In the police world a false alarm was probably the best sort of alarm of all.

"And it isn't an ancient Greek."

"No, Doctor," said Sloan stolidly. "I didn't think it was."

"The Greeks always put an obol between the teeth of the dead to pay Charon, the ferryman, his fare."

"Did they, Doctor?" There was only one thing worse than a pathologist in a bad mood: a pathologist in a playful mood.

"Nowadays," said Dr. Dabbe with mock gravity, "we are all ferried across the River of Death on the National Health."

"So it's not an ancient Greek," began Sloan encouragingly. He was in a hurry even if the doctor wasn't.

"I'm afraid not," said Dabbe. "I'm afraid it's not ancient anything."

"That's what young Dr. Latimer thought," offered Sloan, who had spoken to the general practitioner.

"Latimer? Don't know him."

"Just been appointed to Dr. Tarde's old practice. Shouldn't think he's been here above ten minutes."

"Taken their time, haven't they?" said the pathologist.

"Why, Doctor?"

"Well, it must be a good couple of months since Dr. Tarde went."

"June," said Sloan.

19

"Poor old Henry," said Dabbe. "Now, there was a good fellow. Pint sized, but a darn good doctor. You could have knocked me down with a feather when I heard about him. Last person on earth I should have said to have done a thing like that."

"This skeleton," said Sloan, keeping to the point. "It's not recent surely, Doctor, is it? Not when you've only got the bones . . ."

"Praise-God Barebones," murmured Dabbe irrelevantly.

"I beg your pardon, Doctor . . ."

"One of Cromwell's mob, Inspector."

"So," said Sloan heavily, "you think we should be taking an interest?"

"I do, Sloan."

Sloan got out his notebook. "No chance of it being archeological at all?"

The pathologist shook his head. "I can't date it exactly for you down here in a bad light but I'd say it's definitely within your hundred year limit."

Inspector Sloan sighed. "The bombing, then, I suppose . . ."

"Perhaps."

Detective Inspector Sloan waved an arm. "The whole of this corner looks as if it caught a proper packet. The house came down on top of him, I expect."

"Perhaps," said the pathologist again. "Looking at the skull generally I'd say it hadn't been lying here more than—say—thirty years. So that part would fit. . . ."

"Something else doesn't then?" responded Sloan promptly.

"Don't rush me, Sloan."

"But . . ."

"I haven't seen the rest of the skeleton yet," temporised Dabbe.

"But . . ." said Sloan again.

"But when I have I'll be able to tell you a lot more." He straightened up. "You can bring on the resurrection men now, Inspector."

Sloan beckoned in the direction of the ladder and

two young policemen materialized out of the gloom beyond the arc lights. They were carrying spades.

"Trowels would have been better," growled Dabbe. "It's not that deep in the ground." He waved towards his own assistant, a perennially silent man called Burns, who had been lurking in the shadows. "We'll have some soil samples, please, and some measurements."

Sloan stood by, watching, while the pathologist superintended the digging policemen. What was it that Dr. Dabbe had called them? Resurrection men? He meant Burke and Hare. Sloan took another look at the skull. The anatomists wouldn't have had any use for that. Not now, they wouldn't.

"Gently does it, Constable. The scapula should be about there—ah, yes, that's it. Those are ribs. Now take your spade away while I have another look." Dabbe grunted and then stood back. "Right, carry on."

Sloan murmured "The deceased's age, Doctor . . ."

"Age?" said Dabbe. "Not young. Not old. I'll tell you when I've had a better look. I really need to see the wrists and hips."

Sloan nodded. "The age will be a help." It made a report more tidy, did a stated age.

"Good teeth," observed the pathologist, just as Dr. William Latimer had done. "Mostly present. That'll perhaps be how you'll get onto the identity."

"After all these year?"

Dabbe nodded. "It'll be difficult enough. I can see that."

"Still," Sloan looked round the site, "people often sheltered in their cellars in the bombing. They must have done."

"Careful with that spade, man," adjured the pathologist suddenly. "You're not digging a trench for sweet peas, you know."

Both constables were sweating now. Behind and beyond them the embers of a fire still glowed visibly. That would have been where the men had burnt the smaller branches of the uprooted elm tree earlier in the day. Sloan had been told about that. And about the workmen who had been reluctant to leave the site. From the

21

sound of things they had adjourned to the Rose and Crown. Every now and then he could hear a burst of confused singing from that direction.

The pathologist was back on his knees beside the skeleton now, his hands getting in the way of the two spades.

"Ah," he said suddenly, "the humerus. Now you can expect the rest of that arm about here."

One of the constables obediently applied his implement to the spot. Gradually, ever so gradually, the exposed bones were taking the shape of a complete skeleton.

"If it's lying flat," said the pathologist to the second constable, "you should be getting near the pelvic girdle your side."

"It's funny, Doctor, isn't it," murmured Sloan mildly, "when you come to think of it that it should be lying absolutely flat. . . ."

"If you ask me, Sloan," the pathologist grunted, "I should say it's funnier still that it should be lying flat on its back so . . ."

"So neatly?" supplied Sloan.

Dabbe frowned. "I wouldn't have said it was usual with a crush injury. Blast, perhaps."

The whole of the top of the skeleton was visible now. The pathologist paused and took a good look at it.

"If," said Dr. Dabbe, after a long moment, "it was buried by falling masonry then it was without breaking a single rib. There's the rib cage there absolutely complete."

"Gas?" suggested Sloan suddenly. "I've heard that that happened. The bomb burst the domestic gas supply and bob's your uncle. The other injuries don't matter then."

The pathologist grimaced. "I can't tell you that. Not now. Not just from this."

"No." Sloan stepped back a pace. "There's the earth, of course."

"That'll tell us a thing or two. Burns can start working on that."

"All good Calleshire clay, I expect," said Sloan, "if my garden is anything to go by. Just the job for roses."

22

Though roses seemed a far cry from the scarified rubble of the site.

Suddenly there was a distant gust of singing. It reached them quite clearly over the still evening air.

"Merriment?" enquired Dabbe sardonically. "In St. Luke's on a Monday evening?"

Sloan said he thought it was the Irish labourers from the site conducting a wake for their lost overtime in the Rose and Crown.

"Much more likely," said Dabbe. Suddenly he bent down. The constable on his left had just cleared the earth away from the farther hip bone. "Iliac crest coming up now."

"Ah," said Sloan.

"And it's not quite united," said the pathologist. "Very nearly, but not quite."

"And that means . . ."

"It usually becomes united between about twenty-two and twenty-five." Dabbe pointed. "Look here, Sloan, do you see?"

The police inspector crouched beside him and nodded.

"Union is still incomplete, Sloan, so the deceased, whoever they were, wasn't much more than twenty when they died."

"Thank you," said Sloan drily. "That will give us something to work on . . ."

"It's a European-type skull . . ."

"So will that . . ."

"And unless I'm very much mistaken, Inspector, it was female."

Detective Inspector Sloan permitted himself a smile. "Free, white, and not more than twenty-five, in fact, Doctor . . ."

"My wife says women are never free." Dabbe indicated a still-covered patch of earth to one of the digging constables. "You'll find a femur under that, my lad, if you go carefully. Unless she was one-legged, of course."

"Yes, sir." Dutifully.

"She'll not have been over tall. Her feet'll be about here."

The constables went on digging and Detective Inspec-

23

tor Sloan peered down at the remains. In the last half hour they had progressed from being "a skeleton" to "the deceased" and now to "her."

That was pathology for you.

But Sloan hadn't time for semantics. "It isn't going to be easy," he said, "putting a name to her after all these years . . ."

"No fractures in the lower limbs either," reported the pathologist, still following his own line of thinking.

"Odd that," said Sloan. He began to shiver a bit. It really was beginning to get quite cold out here now. And he would have to stay here until the police photographers, Dyson and Williams, arrived. What was keeping them? he wondered. Beyond the restricting glow of the arc lights an autumn mist was hovering. He wouldn't be surprised if that didn't close in on them soon.

"Sloan!" called out Dabbe. "Come and take a look at this, will you?"

Obediently the police inspector dropped to his knees beside the pathologist and craned his neck over the narrow, gravelike trench.

"See this?" Dr. Dabbe pointed with a long probe to a small indeterminate mass muddled up with the earth in the pelvic girdle. "Do you know what I think this is? I can't tell you for sure until I've seen it in the lab but . . ."

"I think I can guess," said Sloan slowly.

"A foetus," said Dabbe. "See that Flash Harry takes a good picture, won't you?"

Sloan stirred. "So she was pregnant when she died then, was she, Doctor?" Flash Harry was Dyson's nickname. Police Photographer was his proper title.

'For what it's worth. It'll maybe help with the identification, that's all."

"Poor woman," he said suddenly. "Let's hope she never knew what hit her."

"Aye," said the pathologist, not without compassion.

They both stared down at the pathetic collection of bones lying there in the soil and rubble and rudely exposed to their clinical and legal gaze. To Sloan it didn't seem possible that they could properly be described as "woman with child."

But they could.

For the first—but by no means the last—time someone besides Mick the Irishman wished that his pickaxe had not struck just where it had.

*If in doubt, the advice of a coal merchant
should be sought*

3

A man sat in an office in Berebury and thumbed a
piece of paper. It carried all the relevant information so
far known about the skeleton in Lamb Lane, Berebury.

The man was Superintendent Leeyes and he was sitting at his desk in Berebury Police Station. It was nine
o'clock on the Tuesday morning. Detective Inspector
Sloan had been summoned to his presence as soon as he
had set foot inside the police station.

"What's all this, Sloan?"

"What you might call a Records job, I suppose, sir."
Sloan didn't see a lot of hope that it could be shunted
onto someone else but it was always worth a try. "The
pathologist says the body's been dead between twenty-
five and thirty years . . ."

"Thirty years?" said Leeyes lugubriously. "That
makes a change from the day before yesterday's fatal
road traffic accident and today's suicide."

"Yes, sir." Sloan could have done without any of
them actually.

The superintendent waved the paper in front of him.
"It's a pity it wasn't just that bit older and then we
might have got him to stretch it a bit."

"Stretch it, sir?" Cautiously.

"Call it a hundred years old, Sloan, and we don't
need to bother, do we?"

"N . . . no, sir, I suppose not." For a wild moment
Sloan toyed with the idea of trying to explain to the
superintendent that forensic medicine—the pathology
of injury—was a neutral science: and then thought better of it.

"Twenty-five to thirty years," said Leeyes.

"Thirty years," said Sloan, frowning, "would make it somewhere in the war . . ."

"Well done," said his superior officer kindly. "And seeing as how it's been found on an old bomb site, I shouldn't be at all surprised myself if it wasn't a leftover bomb casualty."

"No, sir."

"Though, Sloan, there was a civilisation which buried their dead under their houses. In Cyprus, it was." The superintendent was given to attending adult education classes and was the possessor of sundry items of totally unrelated knowledge.

"Really, sir?"

"Bit niffy, I should have thought myself but there's no accounting for habit." He pushed his chair back and walked across to the window. And groaned.

Once upon a time the superintendent had been able to look out of his window with equanimity. His office was on the first floor of the Berebury Police Station which was in the Market Square. It enjoyed a view across to the other side of the square. Until last June this had mattered not at all. The view had included the Willow Pattern Tea Rooms, an inoffensive establishment run by two inoffensive maiden ladies, the Misses Simpkin.

Since June however there had been changes. One of the Misses Simpkin had gone to Heaven and the other to Bournemouth and a new owner had taken over. The Willow Pattern Tea Rooms had been renamed Dick's Dive and the younger generation had moved in.

It was the younger generation which so disturbed the superintendent.

"Look at them, Sloan." He groaned again. "Just look at them. Dirty. Lazy. Long-haired . . ."

"Yes, sir. This body, sir. In Lamb Lane."

He turned. "It's just a leftover."

"Yes, sir."

"You won't remember, Sloan," said Leeyes loftily, "but that sort of thing did happen."

"I know they will come across unexploded bombs on Luston Moor, sir. I had to give a hand with the traffic once when they found one."

"Same idea," said Leeyes generally. "Leftovers. Like on the golf course. I wrote to the Committee about it only the other day."

"Really, sir?"

"Asked them if they could remove the Danaert wire from behind the ninth green now that the danger of German invasion appears to have receded. That should shake 'em."

"Yes, sir. I'm sure it will. Now about this woman . . ."

"Was she married?"

Sloan started. "I don't know, sir. There's only the skeleton, you know."

"Wedding ring," snapped Leeyes. "Third finger, left hand. Old English custom."

"Yes, sir. Of course, sir. I will make enquiries. And then see what sort of records we've got downstairs."

"The wrong sort," rejoined Leeyes gloomily. "Bound to be. A note of everyone who's ridden a bicycle without a rear light for the last fifty years or who parked their horse and cart badly and nothing more useful." In a flash the superintendent was astride another hobby horse. "That's the trouble with records. You never know which to keep. File one lot and you've got them cluttering up the place for years. Chuck 'em out and someone wants them the next morning."

"Yes, sir." No one could say that the prospect of a Records job carried much appeal to a working detective inspector. "So what you want me to do now is to find out who she is."

"Was."

"Yes, sir."

"And you'd better do it with the speed of light, Sloan, because of the building works." Leeyes left the window and came back to his desk. "I've had someone onto me already about that. Name of Garton."

"That'll be the builder."

"He says this has put them behind schedule right at the beginning of the job. They've got plant and machinery itching to get at the place and men held up."

"I'll see what I can do," promised Sloan. "Dr. Dabbe's doing the official post-mortem this morning." He stood up to go. "I'll need someone with me."

"Crosby."

"Gelven," suggested Sloan quickly. "What about Sergeant Gelven?"

"Crosby," countered the superintendent magnanimously. "You can have Detective Constable Crosby."

Inspector Sloan sighed. "Sergeant Gelven's a good man."

"I know. That's why I'd better have him keeping an eye on Dick's Dive while you're busy. Lord knows what's going on in there. Besides, Crosby can be spared. Easily."

"Yes, sir."

"And I don't see that he can do any harm on a case like this."

"I'm sure I hope not," muttered Sloan.

"Open and shut," said Leeyes. "That's what it'll be."

Just as Detective Inspector Sloan's day was by now well under way, so was Dr. Latimer's. He had finished his morning surgery and was studying the visiting list for the day—the Tuesday—put on his desk in front of him by Miss Tyrell.

"I'll go to Farnely Terrace first," he said, "to see how little Billy Nicholls is now. Unless anything more urgent has come in . . ."

"No, Doctor. Not so far." Miss Tyrell ran her finger down the list. "Jane Appleby sounds to be in a bit of a state but not urgently, if you know what I mean. Mr. Smith will just be having you on, whatever he says the matter is."

"Will he indeed?' said William grimly.

"And watch Mrs. Reddley."

"Oh?"

"Neurotic as they come," said Miss Tyrell succinctly. "She'll waste your whole morning, if you're not careful. And don't forget Mrs. Caldwell. Just a routine call at the moment."

William wasn't likely to forget Mrs. Caldwell. She looked like being his first maternity case in Berebury.

"What shall I tell Mr. Hodge if he rings, Doctor?"

"That his X ray shows a large ulcer and he'd better come to see me this evening." William stowed the list away in his pocket. "I might call in on him myself if I have the time."

"That just leaves Anthea Garton then," said Miss Tyrell. "Can you fit her in after luncheon? We don't want her in the surgery with a rash."

'I expect I can. Tell her to come at two."

"Though if it's only a rash that young woman's got," said Miss Tyrell, "she can be thankful the way she's spending her time."

"Really?" William wasn't paying much attention.

"If her skirts get any shorter this winter," said Miss Tyrell, a steely glint coming into her eye, "her chilblains ought to make medical history."

William grinned. "There's one good thing, though. You aren't going to have your noise from over there on the bomb site just yet after all . . ."

"Oh?"

William told her about the skeleton.

Her head came up alertly. "Over there? Are you sure?"

"Quite sure," said William. He asked her who used to live in the bombed houses opposite. "Can you remember?"

"There were four families," she said, frowning slightly. "Two on each side of the corner. Some people called Masters and Draycott lived in the Conway Street ones. The other two were in Lamb Lane. They were called Waite and . . . and Crowther. Yes, Crowther. That was the name. The bomb hit the corner."

"Where were you at the time?" asked William a little diffidently. Miss Tyrell's age was something he had not so far fathomed and he didn't want her to think him curious.

"Under there, Doctor," she said in a very dry voice indeed. She pointed to the heavy oak desk in the consulting room; a desk that, like everything else about Field House, seemed to go with the practice.

William, who had been sitting at the desk, for some reason immediately withdrew his feet from under it.

"So the third house along from this end . . . let me see now . . . that would have been the Waites'?"

"That's right, Doctor," said Miss Tyrell, nodding. "The Waites' house."

No one could have described Detective Constable Crosby as a comfort to have around. Indeed, Sergeant Gelven usually referred to him as the defective constable.

"St. Luke's, sir? What have we got to go down there for?"

"A job," said Sloan briefly. "And it's only the other side of town. Not Darkest Africa. So get moving."

No sooner were the words out of his mouth than he wished he hadn't spoken. Young, brash, and the despair of all the ranks above him in the police hierarchy, Detective Constable Crosby had so far shown enthusiasm for only one thing.

Driving fast cars fast.

"What sort of job, sir?" he asked, slipping the police car round an articulated lorry and a motorcycle just— but only just—before a large trade van used their road space.

"Look out, you fool!"

"Plenty of room, sir. It's a good road."

It was just as well it was. Crosby took the next corner in a manner calculated to bring the heart to the mouth—and in a way which made at least one watching pedestrian resolve to write to the Home Secretary.

"They all say that," muttered Sloan irritably, "but I don't want to die yet, even if you do." He subsided uneasily back in the passenger seat. "This job has waited thirty years for us, Crosby. Another thirty minutes isn't going to make a lot of difference."

From what he could make of the case at first sight another thirty days wasn't going to make a lot of difference either.

"Just a skeleton in the ruins of a cellar. That's all we've got to go on, Crosby."

"Yes, sir."

"Not buried deep but definitely underground. At least," he corrected himself carefully, "under something. Bomb rubble, perhaps. It hasn't been disturbed

32

for a long time and it's what you might call settled like earth now."

Crosby seemed to be preoccupied with double declutching.

"The pathologist wasn't happy about the way the skeleton was lying though," went on Sloan. "It didn't have the look of accidental burial about it."

"This clutch is a bit sticky, sir."

"You don't say." There was a legend in Berebury Police Station that Constable Crosby's promotion out of the uniformed branch had stemmed entirely from some typist's error: and that somewhere there languished on a lonely beat a man with a name nearly the same. Today Sloan could well believe it.

The police car turned into Conway Street just as Dr. William Latimer left Field House and set off on his morning visiting round. They saw his car go down the road.

"Dr. Latimer," persisted Sloan, "says there were some young archeologists working on the site over the weekend and I know there's been a fair bit of squabbling about the redevelopment because I've read about it in the local paper."

"Yes, sir." Crosby slowed down just short of the monstrous yellow machine that had plucked up the tree yesterday, and pointed. "Shouldn't be on the road at all, sir, that thing shouldn't."

"I don't suppose," said Sloan mildly, "that he wants to be on the road. I expect where he wants to be is on the site and we won't let him." He looked round. "There's a man called Cresswell on duty somewhere."

"He's over there, sir. Near the entrance."

Sloan turned. Entrance was rather a strong word for the gap in the chestnut fencing which constituted the way into the site.

In the daylight it was still possible to see where the doors of the four demolished houses had been. The stone of threshold was usually a substantial affair—it occurred to Sloan, seeing them for the first time isolated as they were—that there was probably a very primitive reason for this. In each case here it had survived

33

the bombing and subsequent demolition. The gap in the fencing, though, was wide enough for machinery and a small army of men to come through.

Police Constable Cresswell was making no attempt to block it.

He was just standing there.

But it was enough.

Sloan knew how it would be. The deceptively casual stroll towards the first man who tried to walk through, followed by the polite negative. The whole strength of the British police system was exemplified by that very casualness and that politeness.

Out on the road was the man whom he guessed was Burrows, the site foreman. He was talking to two other men.

They all greeted Sloan eagerly.

"Ah, Inspector . . ." One of them—the tallest—came forward with a brisk step. "I'm Mark Reddley. We're the site developers here—and this is Garton. It's Garton's firm who are building here."

"Trying to build, you mean," said Garton ruefully, "until this business last night put a stopper on it. Burrows here, my foreman, told us about it and so we came round."

Garton was shorter than Reddley. He was middle-aged and harassed-looking as if he wasted much time.

He came to the point at once. "How long do you need here, Inspector?"

"I couldn't say, sir. Not yet. We don't know a great deal about the skeleton yet."

Garton's head came up with a jerk. "Do you need to, Inspector? After all this time?"

"Of course it doesn't matter who it was," interrupted Reddley impatiently. "What matters is that it's been taken away now and I should have thought that means that we could get cracking on the site."

"Not until we've completed our investigations, sir," said Sloan. He could tell that Reddley wasn't used to being held up. "We'll be as quick as we can."

The developer waved his rolled plans, unappeased. "Time's money, Inspector."

"Very likely, sir," he said. Reddley's might very well

be. Detective Inspector Sloan's wasn't. Sloan's time and money didn't come into anyone's calculations. That was what justice was about.

"It's not all that different from being held up by a sharp attack of frost, I suppose," said Garton,. the builder, more philosophically. "That right, Burrows?"

"Yes, Mr. Garton," responded the foreman. "Or bricks. I've known that happen."

"It still costs money," said Reddley flatly. "And the longer it takes, the more it costs."

"We appreciate that all right, sir," said Sloan, "but the coroner must be informed and . . ."

"And someone always has to pay in the end," said Reddley meaningly.

"Just a minute." Garton was starting to look distinctly uneasy. "Just a minute. This is the sort of thing that could happen to anyone . . ."

"I hope not, gentlemen," intervened Sloan firmly. "It's not every day that a skeleton turns up."

"It's not the skeleton," retorted Reddley. "It's the delay. All these men and machines laid on ready to work and a policeman stopping them doing it. Somebody's got to pay."

Sloan took a step towards Constable Cresswell and the gap in the fence.

"You'll have to get someone to read the small print in your contract for you both, won't you?" He'd been in the force too long to confuse civil law with criminal law and was wise enough never to give an opinion of the former. Besides, the law of contract was quite tortuous enough without the police coming into it. He stepped over the rubble and called back over his shoulder, "There's bound to be a clause about enemy action in it. There almost always is."

This was clearly a new thought to both men.

Detective Constable Crosby followed close on Sloan's heels, grinning. "You can see them both working that one out, sir, only they can't quite remember in whose favour enemy action would be."

"Nobody's, Crosby," Sloan reminded him soberly. "Ever."

35

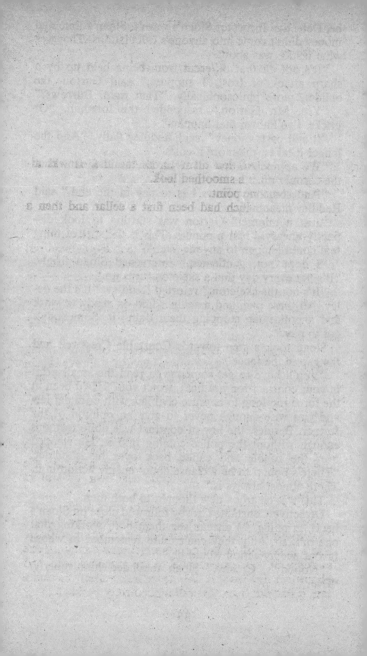

4

P.C. Cresswell led them across the site. It was already taking on a smoothed look.

Except at one point.

The point which had been first a cellar and then a tomb.

"We've had the press here, sir," said Cresswell. "I didn't know quite how you would feel about them but seeing as how I understand it's a question of identification I didn't know but that you might think a bit of publicity might come in handy."

"Found," murmured Sloan absently. "One woman."

"Yes, sir." P.C. Cresswell moved ahead. "The ladder's over here, sir."

The ladder was leaning against the only remaining wall of the cellar. Sloan took his bearings all over again in daylight and decided that it had been an outside wall with solid earth on the other side—the solid earth of the garden, in fact. The side of the cellar facing the street had been shored up a little from the inside—presumably to keep the pavement intact. The two walls which were common to the houses on either side had disintegrated completely. You could not step into the cellar of what had been the house next door without let or hindrance.

But could you have done so thirty years ago?

Sloan stopped and examined the rubble. He thought he could make out the remains of an old party wall. He had a good look at the trench which had contained the skeleton. It was lying parallel to the remaining wall and about two feet from it. Whatever had buried the skeleton, it had not been the wall immediately beside it.

37

"Lying there for shelter, sir?" suggested Crosby. "Along the ground under the wall . . ."

"Perhaps," said Sloan.

If so, the wall hadn't given enough protection when the whole house—when all four houses—came tumbling down on the top of the cellar.

He turned and regarded the other excavation—the one made by the archeologists of last weekend. Saxon remains, wasn't it, that Dr. Latimer had said that they had been looking for?

The little trenches of the archeologists followed an entirely different pattern from those of the remains of the Conway Street and Lamb Lane houses. Sloan wondered idly what cataclysmic event had brought the Saxon settlement in Berebury—if there ever had been one—to an end. Before you had High Explosives to hand, so to speak. He sighed. He supposed they, too, had had their enemies.

Everyone had enemies.

Even Saxons.

Perhaps especially Saxons.

Crosby inadvertently dislodged a piece of broken brick with his shoe. It went clattering down into the shallow trench that had been the unknown woman's grave.

Perhaps, thought Sloan, still considering, the Saxon settlement here had ended not with the wail of warning and the crash-bang of weaponry but with a whimper.

He didn't know.

He wasn't an historian.

Fire and flood and human aggression were enemies common to all history. Perhaps it didn't matter very much in the long run which you succumbed to. And they were all of them better than some diseases he'd seen.

"Sir . . ." Constable Crosby interrupted his reverie.

"Well?" Perhaps this woman was history, too. Lying waiting for some archeologist not yet born to come along and disinter her bones and her history.

"I reckon she took shelter under the stairs." Crosby pointed to the remains of the wall. "Look, sir, you can see where the staircase would have been."

38

"Yes." Sloan stirred unwillingly. She had been found a hundred years too soon. That was her trouble. Better by far if she had been undisturbed until she was more definitely history.

"So she comes down and gets under the stairs," said Crosby, serenely untroubled by thoughts of the past, ending lamely, "only it didn't do her a lot of good, did it, sir?"

"No." The site looked bleak enough in all conscience now. What it must have looked like just after the bombing was beyond Sloan's imagining. "No, it didn't do her a lot of good. The first question, Crosby, is whether it did anyone else any harm at the same time."

"Beg pardon, sir?"

Sloan spelled it out for him. "Was she alone, man, or was anyone else buried at the same time?"

Crosby scratched his head. "I hadn't thought of that, sir."

"We shall have to make sure." Sloan dropped to his knees, noting, just as Dr. Latimer had done, the other set of peg marks the archeologists had left behind. "I wonder what made them change their minds?"

If there really were archeological remains about he would have to check with the Curator of the Berebury Museum, Mr. Esmond Fowkes, before any more digging was done. Sloan knew him by repute: a man to whom the past was more important than the present.

He paced out the small cellar and was glad neither Crosby nor Cresswell had asked him why it was important to find anyone else. If any other bodies were here they were buried in earth and if they were found they would later be reburied in earth . . .

Earth to earth, dust to . . .

"Blast," said Sloan enigmatically.

"Sir?"

"I expect that's what killed her without breaking any bones."

"Yes, sir."

They spent the next half hour in going over the remains of the cellar, gleaning only the knowledge that the floor was compounded of an indeterminate mixture of broken brick and mortar churned with Calleshire clay. Where the rubble ended and the earth began, it was impossible to say.

Garton, the harassed-looking builder, and the more contained developer, Reddley, were still in the road talking.

"There is something you two could tell me, gentlemen," said Sloan, "that might save a bit of time. . . ."

"What's that, Inspector?" Reddley turned quickly. "Anything that will save time. . . ."

"This site—who does it belong to?"

"Gilbert Hodge," said Garton immediately. "Gilbert Hodge of Glebe Street."

Sloan wrote that down. "And what sort of building is to be put here?"

"The development"—Reddley waved the plans which he still carried in his hand—"is for shops on the ground floor and office space above."

"Offices out here?" Sloan looked around. "This far out?"

The developer smiled. "It can't stay that way, you know, forever. It won't be far out soon."

Garton tugged at his ear. "I know what you mean, Inspector, and I must say I think it's a pity all the same. There are some nice old houses in this part of the town."

"If you had to pay rent for some of those offices and shops in the High Street," declared Reddley, "you'd want something less expensive pretty quickly. Farsighted chap, old Gilbert Hodge."

"Is he?" enquired Sloan.

"He bought up a lot of this sort of derelict bomb site immediately after the war. Reckoned he was going to make on it in the long run." Reddley tapped his plans again. "I should say he hasn't lost on this one."

"'Tisn't built yet," pointed out Garton obstinately.

"You mean"—Sloan attempted to sort out the police wheat from the commercial chaff—"that this Gilbert Hodge didn't own these houses when they were bombed in the war?"

"Mr. Hodge," said Garton respectfully, "is a purely postwar enterprise. What he has done began with his gratuity."

"Who owned them before?"

"I couldn't say, Inspector." He jerked his thumb over his shoulder. "Try the doctor's receptionist. She'll know. She knows everything in these parts. Face like the back of a bus but a memory like an elephant."

"Much more important," agreed Sloan gravely. Faces were deceptive things. Until you considered them all impartially as masks you couldn't really be said to be a policeman. Then you knew you had first always to get behind the mask. . . .

Mr. Esmond Fowkes, the Curator of the Berebury Museum, was a short man with a neat white spade beard. He was down at the Lamb Lane site within minutes of getting Sloan's message. He certainly wanted to be present if there was going to be any further digging.

"The Saxon excavation . . ." began Sloan, waving an arm towards the cellar.

"Ah! Most disappointing."

"You thought . . ."

"Thought? I was sure, Inspector. Ready to stake my reputation on there being a Saxon settlement there."

"But . . ."

"It was all most unfortunate." The little man was determined to have his say. "You see, I had to be in London last weekend. No time. They were going to start building work first thing on Monday morning, you know . . . "

Sloan said he knew.

"So I had to drum up help quickly. I got Colin Rigden to arrange the actual dig. He's a good lad. But they found nothing at all, I'm afraid."

"Nothing Saxon," pointed out Sloan, who was a policeman and not an archeologist.

"Not a thing," declared Fowkes, the Museum Curator. "And I could have sworn they would. There's a fair bit of Saxon stuff in Berebury, you know, and I took my bearings from a known settlement. A late one."

"Late?" enquired Sloan carefully. "How late?"

Fowkes waved a hand. "Ninth century."

Crosby smothered a snort.

Only just.

"Quite so," said Sloan swiftly.

"And when they ran the new gas main down Lamb Lane—you can see their trench over there—one of the workmen came up with a disc brooch. Same date. Lovely piece. Silver niellosed."

"Really, sir?"

"Saxon art is a study of its own . . ."

"I'm sure it is, sir," said Sloan hastily.

"Can't understand it at all." Fowkes frowned. "I still think there should have been something here."

"Something Saxon," interposed Sloan.

There had, after all, been something there all right.

"I worked it out most carefully. Sat up most of the night, if you must know, Inspector."

"Did you, sir?"

"I only got wind of the work starting so soon on the Thursday. You know what it is. We have all this elaborate business of someone in the Council Office giving us Museum people fair warning, and when it comes to the point some little office girl forgets and the whole machinery breaks down."

"Yes, sir." Their instructions at the police station had been equally firm. Ever since a police constable had put a piece of perfect Roman glass in the dustbin. Esmond Fowkes, though small, had torn a stripe off no less a person than the Chief Constable. "How did you happen to hear in the end?"

"I got a whisper in the Goat and Compasses, if you must know."

Sloan nodded. He knew that pub, all right. Just off the Market Square.

"Then I got straight on to Garton. Blew him up good and proper, I did . . ."

Sloan could well imagine it. A mere builder would be nothing to a man who had presumed to reprimand the Chief Constable.

" . . . but he said Reddley had said he'd notified the Council. Anyway, Garton told me I could do what I liked on the site as long as I'd got it done by eight o'clock on Monday morning."

"But you had to go to London," prompted Sloan. He was anxious to get on. To talk to this receptionist, to find out who used to live here and to clear up the case. Then he could get back to more pressing problems. Like the goings-on in Dick's Dive.

"That's right." Fowkes tugged at his beard. "So I did the paper work Thursday night, and Friday I got the caretaker at the Museum to give me a hand with the pegging out. Rigden came along first thing Saturday morning with his team and started digging."

"I see, sir. Now if . . . "

Fowkes shook his head sadly. "This is all a big disappointment to me, Inspector, because of the church."

"The church?"

"I'm doing a monograph for the Calleshire Archeological Society on St. Luke's Church."

"Really, sir?"

The curator waved an arm to take in the whole area. "The one good thing that came out of the bombing."

"And what would that have been, sir?"

"They got St. Luke's Church," he said simply. "Victorian, it was. It all went except for the tower."

Sloan observed that towers always seemed to last well.

"They stood up to blast," said the archeologist academically. "The thick walls and great weight were just the thing for that, though their builders could never have known." He sighed. "But it made them chimney shafts at the same time."

"Chimney shafts, sir?" Sloan changed his weight from one foot to the other. He should have left the site before Mr. Fowkes arrived. He would know another time.

"That's right. Drawing up the flames from the body of the church."

"I see."

"Then the wooden bell frames went and the bells came crashing down."

"That wouldn't help."

"And then you lost your cupola."

"Did you?"

"But afterwards . . ."

"Yes?" Sloan supposed he should be taking an inter-

43

est in anything that happened in St. Luke's after the bombing.

"Afterwards," said Fowkes, "we found a Saxon doorway in the tower of St. Luke's."

"Did you, sir?"

"Together," said Fowkes, "with portions of a Saxon cross of rather rude sculpture. The modern architect often used the lower part of the existing wall if it was sound, you know."

Sloan nodded. "So you wanted to connect the Lamb Lane site with this in your paper, sir?"

"Naturally," He sighed. "And I thought I was on safe ground."

In the event, thought Sloan, the Lamb Lane site hadn't turned out to be safe ground for someone else either.

Whoever she was.

"Perhaps," suggested Sloan, "your original peg marks would have been better after all."

The spade beard came up with a jerk. "My original peg marks, Inspector?"

"Yes, sir. You know. The first set by the wall. Before you moved them."

Fowkes stared at him. "I didn't move them, Inspector. I put them in by the wall."

Scrape and wash the bones and saw in
half across . . .

5

Miss Tyrell answered the policemen's ring at the surgery door of Field House. She was still in her white coat.

"The houses opposite, miss," said Sloan, when he had explained their errand, "can you tell us . . ."

"Draycott, Masters, Waite, and Crowther were the people who used to live there, Inspector."

"Thank you. That's a great help." Sloan scribbled rapidly. "Now, about the actual night of the bombing . . . it was night, I take it, miss?"

She nodded, a faint smile on her lips. "A Wednesday night."

"You remember it well," offered Sloan.

"It's not the sort of thing you forget easily."

Sloan tried again. "What do you remember about it most clearly?"

"The nightingales," she said without hesitation.

"What about them?"

"They wouldn't stop singing." She adjusted her glasses more firmly on the bridge of her nose. "It was quite heartbreaking. They were so lovely—and so unconcerned about all the death and destruction. I've never heard them sing like it . . ."

"A Wednesday, you said it was?" That would give them something to go on. Something that the coroner could write down. For the record.

"That's right. There was a good moon so we guessed—Dr. Tarde and I—that there would be a bad raid. He was on duty at the First Aid Post. I stayed here."

Sloan twisted his pencil. "The moon helped the

planes to see where they were going, I suppose, miss . . ."

Miss Tyrell's thin lips twitched. "What we had that night was worse than that, Inspector. What we had was moon after rain. That's what suited them best."

"Moon after rain?"

"Especially if the moon wasn't too high in the sky. That way," said Miss Tyrell, "the shadows cast by the buildings together with the moonlight reflected from the wet streets gave them all they needed."

"What you might call a Hunter's Moon, miss . . ."

"A Bomber's Moon, Inspector. That's what it was." She looked at him wryly. "Dangerous Moonlight."

Dangerous Moonlight. The phrase rang a bell in Sloan's mind . . . but he couldn't immediately place it. "I see. Now, miss, can you remember if anyone was killed or missing opposite?"

"No," she said positively. "Not there. Corton's had a lot of casualties that night and so did the railway station but there was no one missing at the time from over there."

"The people," he said. "Where were they?"

"In their shelters at the bottom of the garden."

"And they were all right?"

"Oh, yes. Those houses have long narrow gardens, Inspector. There's more land to the site than you'd think at first. And the shelters were at the far end."

"And they all got there in time?"

What in a mellower person might have passed for a smile flitted across Miss Tyrell's face. "Certainly, Inspector. Even Mrs. Crowther."

"Mrs. Crowther?"

"It was a standing joke. Mrs. Crowther was never out of Dr. Tarde's surgery. If it wasn't her rheumatism it was her heart and if it wasn't her heart it was her weight. If you'd listened to all her ailments you'd have thought she couldn't walk a step."

"And?"

"And none of them ever stopped her getting to the shelter first."

"You didn't shelter?"

"Not that night. Sometimes, you know, they were

46

only on their way to Luston. We lie between Luston and France, you see, so you could waste a lot of time in the shelter if you weren't careful."

Sloan regarded the gaunt, rather uncompromising woman in front of him and wondered how the crowd from Dick's Dive would get on under fire; whether they would feel they couldn't spare the time to shelter . . .

"Sometimes, of course, Inspector, they couldn't find Luston . . ."

"The bombs on the Moor," he said suddenly.

"That's right. I believe they're still finding them. Sometimes, of course, they just didn't want to go on—there were guns and searchlights on the Moor—so they bombed us instead, and sometimes," she finished simply, "they just bombed Berebury because they wanted to. Corton's was doing war work, of course. They may have known about that."

Sloan turned the conversation back to the houses opposite. He did it carefully. No one except the police as yet knew that the skeleton had been female.

"You're sure no one was killed or missing over there?"

"Oh, yes, Inspector. I should have known, you see. They were all patients here."

Sloan's spirits sank. If the dead woman had been just a passer-by taking shelter in the nearest house in a bad raid their task might well be a hopeless one . . .

"The Waites, Miss Tyrell. Do you remember them?"

"Certainly, Inspector. They were a nice old couple."

"Family?"

"Two sons."

"No daughters?"

"No."

"Mr. and Mrs. Waite—are they still alive?"

She shook her head. "No. They were getting on in the war, you know. Losing their house didn't help either. The man went first—heart failure"—Miss Tyrell obviously had a card-index brain—"and then his wife. Chronic nephritis, I think she died from. They were pleasant people. You know—decent and undemanding."

Sloan nodded. From a doctor's receptionist the word "undemanding" was high compliment.

"The Waites' sons," he said. "What sort of age would they have been in the war?"

"Army age," responded Miss Tyrell promptly. "Harold—that was the elder one—did well. He ended up as a sergeant in the West Calleshires. The younger boy—Leslie—went off into the Navy if I remember rightly, though I can't imagine why. They weren't seafaring people at all."

"Didn't want to be pushed about by his elder brother in the West Calleshires, I expect." Sloan grinned. "I guess, miss, he made the mistake of thinking they didn't have sergeants in the Navy."

"Perhaps, Inspector."

"What happened to them?"

"They both came back but after that I'm not very sure. I don't think Berebury was ever the same for them, you know, after the family house went. They both moved away when the old people died, what with there being no real home here any more to speak of . . ."

Sloan turned and looked out the window at the empty space that had been number one, Lamb Lane. "I can quite understand that, miss. Where did they go to?"

"Harold went to Luston, I think, to work there. He'd been with Corton's before the war but he was one of those who couldn't settle afterwards. There were quite a few of them, you know."

"I can believe that, miss." Sloan himself wasn't at all sure that he would have settled down to a dull routine job in Berebury after five years in the Army in wartime. "Did he have an exciting war, then?"

"Dunkirk, Tobruk, and then the Second Front," said Miss Tyrell astringently. "Corton's seemed too big a change for him after that. He came to see Dr. Tarde quite often about then and I think he advised him to move."

"Did he now?" murmured Sloan absently. "That's interesting."

"Thought perhaps he should get away. A complete

48

change, you know, instead of trying to pick up the broken threads."

"Did that do the trick?"

"I never heard, Inspector. He certainly didn't come back to Berebury, that's all I know."

"And the younger son? Leslie, did you say his name was?"

"Leslie Waite." Miss Tyrell sniffed. "When he came out of the Navy the only thing he couldn't settle to was work. Work in any shape or form. Never had. Never could."

"And what became of him?" enquired Sloan with genuine interest. He himself had been sternly brought up to "Go to the ant, thou sluggard: consider her ways and be wise" and occasionally—when sorely overworked—wondered what would have happened to him if he hadn't. It was an eternally tantalising line of thought and he wasn't entirely convinced that the ants had it.

"I have an idea that he settled Kinnisport way. Something," Miss Tyrell said vaguely, "to do with boats, but I'm not sure what. He wasn't cut out for success anyway."

Sloan glanced out of the window again. The driver of the articulated machine in the road was still sitting in his cab, reading his paper, totally undisturbed by the delay. Mark Reddley and the man Garton didn't seem quite so calm. Even at this distance it was possible to see that they were not entirely happy. While he watched them they parted abruptly and drove off in their respective cars. Mr. Esmond Fowkes on the other hand looked quite absorbed. Sloan could see him pottering happily about the site.

"Was either son married, Miss Tyrell, at the time of the bombing?" He'd been lucky to find this woman. She was a great time saver.

"No," she said decisively. "I'm sure they weren't. Harold married afterwards. When he came home. I remember the wedding quite well. He married the daughter of the draper in Shepherd Street. Well set up girl. Used to teach in the Sunday school."

"And Leslie?"

49

"Leslie wasn't married at all while he was here in Berebury that I know of."

"Oh?" Sloan caught her tone, not her choice of of words.

"That is not to say," went on Miss Tyrell censoriously, "that it was for lack of interest in the subject."

"One for the girls?" suggested Sloan lightly.

"Always. From about the age of fourteen he always had one or two of them in tow."

"Every nice girl," observed Sloan, "loves a sailor . . ."

Miss Tyrell looked disapproving. "If you ask me, Inspector, being in the Navy got him out of a lot of difficulties. Those leaves of his . . ."

"Like that, was he?"

"Then he'd go back to his ship and next time it would be someone quite different."

"Inconstant," agreed Sloan, making a note.

Their own next port of call was the police station.

"After the post-mortem," said Sloan to Crosby, as they passed the site, "I reckon we should be able to give the builders the go-ahead."

Which was where he was wrong.

Detective Constable Crosby did, in fact, succeed in getting Harold Waite's address from the Luston Police quite quickly.

"Dead easy, sir. They found him and his wife on the electoral register straight off."

"And his wife?" repeated Sloan. In his experience of all categories of human relationship wives were the most at risk.

"That's what they said, sir. Man and woman, both of the name of Waite living at 24, Bean Street, Luston." Crosby shut his notebook with an audible snap.

"We'll get there now," decided Sloan.

Before the superintendent had time to ask him why he hadn't been.

The kindest thing that could be said about the suburb of Luston where Harold Waite lived was that it was probably awaiting redevelopment. It had not been made more salubrious by the fact that the adjacent suburb had already been razed to the ground and looked as if some particularly vicious war of attrition had been fought to the finish there. The only positive sign of regrowth was a block of flats tottering towards the sky.

That was when they stopped to ask a point duty policeman the way.

"Keep your backs to Babel and you'll soon find it."

"Babel?"

"You strangers here in Luston?"

Sloan nodded.

"I thought so," said the man. "Everyone in Luston knows Babel's what those flats are called. Not really. They're named after the mayor. But everyone calls them Babel. You keep the car so you can't see them and you'll soon be in Bean Street."

"That's something, I suppose," said Sloan unenthusiastically as Crosby turned the car away from the flats and plunged it into a maze of crisscrossed streets of terraced houses.

He was devoutly thankful that he did not live here.

It was all too apparent that Luston—like Topsy—had just growed. He could see how the houses—barracks of industry—had erupted in response to the quick pressures of the Industrial Revolution. There was no method about the layout of the huddled streets, and Bean Street—when they found it—was no different from all the others.

As the police car slowed down outside number twenty-four lace curtains twitched all the way down the street.

A thin, spare woman, her hair scraped well back from a bony forehead, answered their knock. She grudgingly admitted to being Mrs. Waite and that her husband was at home.

"He's just got up, if you must know. Ready for his dinner. He's on the twilight shift this month—he's going to work at five. If he's spared . . ."

She showed them into a front parlour of depressing respectability. It was so clean as to be almost sterile. The dustless grate had been covered with a paper fan of red crepe, pleated to fit the space. It didn't even give a successful illusion of warmth and the whole room had the chill of disuse about it.

51

"Sit down," she said. It was more of a command than an invitation. "And I'll fetch him through."

"Proper home from home, sir, isn't it?" said Crosby chattily as soon as she was gone.

Sloan looked at the uncreased cushions and decided against disturbing them. He wandered instead towards the bay window. There was a large Bible on a lace-covered table there.

"Handy that, sir, isn't it?" observed Crosby.

"Handy?"

"If anyone should be thinking of swearing to anything."

Sloan regarded him for a long moment. "We, Crosby, are a very long way from the swearing stage. And we may never get to it."

"Never mind, sir," said Crosby cheerfully, "at least we're not married to that. Talk about home comforts for the troops . . ."

"Good morning," said Sloan swiftly as Mrs. Waite returned with a middle-aged man in tow. "Mr. Harold Waite?"

"Aye." If Harold Waite was surprised to have a visit from two detectives he did not show it. He was of medium build with a close-cropped Army hairstyle. A small hedge-tear scar ran down the corner of his left forehead. In spite of the middle age, he still had the muscular ready look of a man who worked on his feet as opposed to at a desk.

"We need your help."

"You're welcome. Though I don't know how I can help you . . ." He looked at Sloan enquiringly. "Clara and I lead pretty quiet lives, don't we?"

Mrs. Waite wiped her hands on her apron and said in a flat voice, "We try to keep all Ten Commandments, Inspector."

"Er—good." Sloan hadn't time to work out if they covered all crime. He doubted it. "I'm very glad to hear it," he said to her warmly, "but it's not about that sort of—er—transgression that I've come about . . ."

"Good."

"A skeleton of a young woman has been unearthed on the site of your old family home, Mr. Waite."

52

"In Lamb Lane?"

"That's right."

"Well, I never," said Harold Waite, manifestly surprised. "Fancy that."

"A skeleton?" echoed Clara Waite. "The ways of the Lord are truly mysterious."

"Quite so, madam." Mick the Irishman, Sloan felt, would be the first to agree with her. "It was—er—accidentally revealed by some redevelopment work."

"It was meant," declared Clara Waite in her curious flat monotone.

"Redevelopment?" said Harold Waite promptly. "You mean they've got started at last?"

"They tried," qualified Sloan. "Mark Reddley and Associates . . ."

"Associates? Huh," said Waite. "Bet they're not the same associates as he used to have. He's done well for himself, he has."

"And Garton and Garton, Builders."

"Still trying to please everybody, I suppose."

"Well . . ." Now he came to think of it there had been something placating about Garton.

"You're forgetting Gilbert Hodge," said Waite. "He'll be behind it. He bought the site." Husband and wife exchanged glances. "He's had to wait a long time, hasn't he, Clara, to collect his money?"

"He has," said Clara Waite, not without a certain satisfaction. "Just after the war it was when he put down good money for that old site."

"Did he?" murmured Sloan, making a note.

Waite stirred. "We got married on the strength of it, Inspector. Clara and me. I'd come out of the Army by then."

"And then you left Berebury," pointed out Sloan mildly.

"I did. And I've never regretted it. I've got a good job here at the factory down the road."

"I think I can hear it." Sloan had been conscious of a monotonous low-pitched whine in the background ever since they had got out of the car.

"Hear it?" said Waite blankly. "I can't hear any-

53

thing. No," he said, reverting to Berebury, "I shook it off once and for all in 1946."

"Why?"

Harold Waite looked at him consideringly. "It was never the same place for me after the house was bombed."

"I suppose not."

"Then the old folks went."

"They were taken," interposed Clara Waite in sepulchral tones.

"Quite so," said Sloan.

"This skeleton," said Waite. "Could it have been anything to do with the war?"

"It could," admitted Sloan cautiously. "The—er—vintage is right."

Mrs. Waite smoothed her apron down over her knees. "You weren't there when the house was bombed, were you, Harry?"

"Square-bashing," said Waite feelingly. "That's what I was doing at the time. And a fat lot of good that did to anybody."

"That's right," said Harry's wife. "He wasn't there."

"This woman, Inspector," said Waite. "Was it someone taking shelter? My parents said it was a bad night, the Wednesday."

"Very bad," chimed in Clara Waite. "I remember it well. But, Inspector, if there had been anyone missing we'd have heard surely, wouldn't we?"

It was at that moment that Sloan caught a glimpse of Harold Waite's expression.

Clara Waite might not have heard of anyone missing.

Harold Waite most certainly had.

6

Dr. Latimer came back to Field House for his morning coffee at much the same time as he had done the day before.

Miss Tyrell was sitting in her own little cubbyhole when he went in. He wondered briefly if she had any sort of separate existence apart from the practice. Now he came to think of it, he didn't even know where she lived—except that it was somewhere near.

"The police have been," she greeted him, "making enquiries about the deceased."

Latimer blinked.

So the bundle of bones, being not archeological, had therefore in police parlance become "someone."

The deceased.

As if they had died yesterday.

"Probably a neighbour or just a passer-by . . ."

"Not a neighbour," said Miss Tyrell definitely.

"I didn't mean old Jackson. I know he's alive and kicking—but what about the other way?"

"Masters and Draycott?"

"That's right. What sort of family did they have?"

"Masters were a young couple with small children at the time and the Draycotts had a daughter who would have been in her twenties then."

"I was wondering if the cellars had been common to both houses . . ."

"Marjorie." Miss Tyrell smiled faintly. "Marjorie Draycott. She isn't your skeleton, Doctor. Far from it. You've met her already."

"I have? When?"

"She's Marjorie Simmonds now."

55

"Mrs. Simmonds! Well, I never. Not the one who's so overweight and worried about it?" There had been positively nothing skeletal about the woman he had in mind. "Yesterday morning's surgery . . ."

"That's right." Miss Tyrell's thin face twitched a trifle acidly. "Fair, fifteen stone, forty-five, five children . . ."

"The classic gall-bladder picture," murmured William academically. It had been really rather interesting to see a textbook case come alive so vividly.

"You gave her a lot of advice . . ."

"I did."

"She won't take it."

"No," agreed William. He sounded apologetic. "I have a duty to give it nevertheless. The choice about taking it is hers. The patients' freehold, you might call it."

Miss Tyrell looked blank.

William hastily went back to the visiting list in front of him. "I've seen Gilbert Hodge. He's agreed to see a surgeon about his ulcer. Will you fix him up with an appointment at the hospital?"

Miss Tyrell snorted. "I didn't think he'd want Vittoria Street even though he's one of the richest men in Berebury. And definitely the meanest," she added. "Long pockets and short arms, that's his trouble."

"He doesn't look well off . . ."

"Don't let that fool you, Doctor. He owns a string of shops, no end of other property and a couple of small businesses and that's all without counting his builders' merchant's yard." She sniffed. "That's not small either. Two acres at least."

"Really?"

"And he started from nothing at all after the war. With his gratuity. First these building things and then property speculation. He gets Mark Reddley to do the developing side and Garton to build." Miss Tyrell's lips tightened. "Before the war, Doctor, all he was was a storeman at Corton's."

"I saw Jane Appleby, too . . ."

Miss Tyrell's face softened momentarily. "A nice girl. Always was. Many's the time I've had her on my knee as a baby."

William took a second look at Miss Tyrell and tried to imagine her in this maternal role.

He failed.

"What about Mrs. Caldwell?" she asked.

"Nothing doing," said William. "Not today, anyway. I might just look round there after supper . . ." Mentioning supper brought Mrs. Milligan—that execrable cook—to his mind. He didn't know how long he could put up with her. He asked how long she'd been with Dr. Tarde before he died.

"Only a month."

"And before that?"

Miss Tyrell's expression eased. "He had Mrs. Cardington. She died in May. She'd been here for years and years. She had a heart attack and went quite suddenly. Of course, she wasn't young any more . . ."

"What about Dr. Tarde's wife?" enquired William. He'd done his business with an executor, a second cousin who was a solicitor somewhere in the North of England. "And children?"

She shook her head. "His wife died soon after they were married. Before my time. They didn't have any children. There was just his niece Margaret." Miss Tyrell pursed her lips. "She liked to be called Margot. She was his wife's sister's girl. She used to spend a fair bit of time here in the old days but she went off one night and didn't come back." The receptionist was still keeping an eye on her notes. "You haven't forgotten that the Caduceus Club meets tonight, Doctor, have you?"

William clapped his hand to his forehead. "I had. Tell me about them again . . ."

"It's a club for all the general practitioners in Berebury," explained Miss Tyrell patiently, "and they've invited you to go along tonight. Caduceus . . ."

"Yes?" said William humbly. It was when classical and historical allusions flew about that he was most conscious of the terrace house from whence he had sprung.

"Caduceus was the name of Mercury's wand. You know, Doctor, the one which has the two snakes twined round it . . ."

57

The only Mercury William Latimer knew to be associated with healing was the small quantity in the bulb of a clinical thermometer but he did not say so.

"The Caduceus Club meets once a month at the Feathers Hotel at 8:30 P.M. That's so that everyone's had a chance to finish their evening surgeries, Doctor."

"I see." William resolved to start his own very sharply indeed. It would take him a little while to find the Feathers for the first time.

When he went out on his visiting round again he noticed that the monster yellow digger was still parked in Lamb Lane. He looked across at the almost deserted site and reflected that the only thing he—and perhaps anyone else—knew for certain about the identity of the skeleton so far was that it wasn't called Marjorie Simmonds née Draycott.

"Good morning, gentlemen." Dr. Dabbe greeted Sloan and Crosby in the post-mortem room of the hospital. "And how have you been getting on?"

"Slowly," said Sloan. "We've seen one of the Waite sons but not the other. And we've had a look at the local paper."

The issue of the Berebury paper for the Friday after the Wednesday could only be described as coyly reticent on the subject of the bombing of Berebury.

"Somewhere in England" had been about as far as the paper had been prepared to go at the time by way of location.

"The community suffered severely" was their spare comment on casualties: "A number of houses were completely demolished" the taut observation by the reporter on damage.

Sloan cleared his throat. "It wasn't a great deal of help to us, Doctor. I should think there was pretty stringent censorship on newspapers at the time."

"Walls have ears," murmured Dr. Dabbe, getting into his surgical gown.

"Be like Dad, keep Mum," Sloan was surprised to hear himself responding.

How from whereabouts in the dim recesses of his own mind had that phrase been dredged up? It must have been lurking there dormant all the long years since

58

the war. He hadn't even known that he knew it, still less remembered it.

Sloan had fingered the fragile wartime paper stacked away in the basement of the newspaper office, read its faded yellow columns and replaced it on the shelf. Probably the next time someone got it out would be for one of those reminiscent newspaper features "Forty-Four Years Ago" . . .

Dr. Dabbe pulled on his rubber gloves, glanced at his assistant, caught his secretary's eye and began dictating . . .

"To Her Majesty's Coroner for West Calleshire, with copies to the Chief Constable and Dr. William Latimer. Head it 'Report on unknown human remains found under the site of 1, Lamb Lane, St. Luke's . . .'"

"Does that mean, Doctor," interrupted Sloan, "that—for the record—the coroner's bound to ask—there was no identity disc on or near the body?"

"It does, Inspector."

"In spite of its being wartime?"

The pathologist grunted. "I assure you that there was no such disc near the neck or either arm nor in the surrounding earth. Burns here checked."

Sloan nodded. There was, apparently, to be no easy way out.

Dabbe waved an arm. "We'll take the little one first, shall we, Inspector?"

Sloan started. "The little one, Doctor?"

"Over here." The pathologist pointed to a separate little pile of bones on another bench. They were grey and discoloured. "There is no doubt, Inspector, about the pregnancy though much of the cartilaginous content has gone, and by Hasse's rule . . ."

"Hasse's rule?"

"That's right. The age of a foetus may be estimated approximately by Hasse's rule."

"Can it?" said Sloan cautiously.

"Up to the fifth month the length in centimetres, the lower limbs being included, equals the square of the age in months, and after the fifth month the length in centimetres equals the age multiplied by five."

"I see, sir," said Sloan impassively. It was all right

for the doctor. He could blind the coroner with science as much as he liked. He didn't have a superintendent breathing down his neck who always wanted to know the reason why. He could see Detective Constable Crosby still struggling to write it all down. He only hoped he got it right. He knew for a fact that Crosby was only up to the sort of mental arithmetic where you took away the number you first thought of.

"I," went on Dr. Dabbe cheerfully, "aided by Hasse's rule, calculate that the foetus was between five and six months advanced at the time of death."

"Quite so." Sloan coughed. "That might very well be a help in identification in the end."

"And it very well might not," retorted the pathologist promptly.

"Oh?"

Dr. Dabbe turned and pointed to the adult skeleton on the other dissection table. "There was something missing from the proximal phalanx of her fourth left metacarpal."

"Her what?"

"Her ring finger," translated Dr. Dabbe.

"No ring?" said Sloan swiftly.

"No. If you ask me, Sloan," said Dr. Dabbe solemnly, "I'd say the baby was on time but the wedding was late. There was no ring in the ground anyway—at least, not when the left arm was unearthed—but as to before . . ."

"I shouldn't have said the body was accessible enough to have been robbed earlier," said Sloan slowly. "If it had been, then I think it would have been found before now."

"A good point," conceded the pathologist. "Quite apart from anything else, of course, Inspector, I must remind you that there would also have been considerable mephitis."

"Mephitis, Doctor?" That was a new one on Sloan. He kept his tone deliberately neutral—in spite of the fact that he always supposed doctors used words such as this on purpose to cut lay people—like patients and policemen—down to size.

The pathologist's eyebrows rippled. He intoned in a

parsonic manner, "A pestilential emanation from the earth, Sloan." The phrase certainly did have a biblical ring about it. "More shortly, stench."

Sloan breathed more easily.

That was a word Constable Crosby could both spell and understand. He heard his sigh of relief.

"Now to the mother . . ." said Dr. Dabbe.

It was Sloan's turn to sigh.

There was the doctor using an ordinary human expression in the medical sense. It was all very confusing and not really very fair. Anything looking less like a mother than the skeleton would have been difficult to imagine . . .

"In my opinion," dictated the pathologist, moving across to the post-mortem table, "the bones are those of a woman aged between twenty-two and twenty-five at the time of death. She was of medium height—five foot five. As you see, Sloan, we have the complete skeleton here so that figure is reached by direct measurement . . ."

That was a relief, thought Sloan. One formula—if it was as complicated as Hasse'—was quite enough to be going on with.

"I can't tell you anything about her build or colouring. The earth in which she was buried was evidently not damp enough for adipocere . . ."

Sloan could see Crosby having a lot of difficulty in spelling that one.

"The teeth are consistent with the age suggested by the state of development of the iliac crest," went on the pathologist. "They were well-looked after and had been treated for caries at early stages."

"That suggests a certain level of income and intelligence," said Sloan, "in those days."

Dectective Constable Crosby, who had a small hole in his left eyetooth, closed his mouth and kept it closed.

"And an interest in her appearance," agreed Dabbe. "Dentist were more . . . aggressive then than now." He peered inside the jaw and called out the state of each tooth. "My secretary will give you the dental picture, Inspector, before you go."

"Thank you, Doctor."

The pathologist acknowledged this gloomily. "I don't know that we're likely to pick up any other clues as to who the poor creature was. Just the teeth and perhaps the pregnancy." He turned his attention back to the rest of the skull. "No fractures. Cranium normal. No fracture or dislocation of the cervical vertebrae." He poked and probed. "No fractures of upper limbs, shoulder blades, sternum—rib cage complete except for . . ." his voice died away as he peered forward.

"Except for what, Doctor?"

"Except for her left fifth rib which appears to have been chipped by something."

"Chipped?"

"Look. The upper aspect has been damaged. There's a bit missing."

"Yesterday's digging," suggetsed Sloan. "After all, they didn't know she was there."

"No." Dabbe shook his head and said firmly, "This is an old chip."

"What does it mean?" asked Sloan.

"Something hit it from an angle." Dabbe picked up the nearest instrument to hand. A wicked-looking bone saw. He reproduced the angle of the chip with the saw. "Like this. See? And whatever did it chipped a bit out of the bone. Interesting."

The pathologist's idea of what was interesting wasn't Sloan's. "That little chip wouldn't have killed her, Doctor, surely? I mean, if the whole house came down on her in an air raid it would have been more than just . . ."

"It's what caused the chip. Not the chip itself. A retractor, Burns, here and here, please."

His assistant moved obediently forward.

With unexpected gentleness Dr. Dabbe adjusted the angle of the rib cage. "Now a light . . ."

Instead of peering between the ribs the pathologist was squinting up under them from where the deceased's stomach had been.

"Mirror," he said tersely.

Burns supplied it.

"Probe."

"Probe."

Dr. Dabbe's head had almost disappeared now. "Forceps."

"Forceps coming."

"Not these, Burns. Give me a Spencer Wells."

Burns selected a different pair. "Spencer Wells, Doctor."

"Got to get a grip," came the muffled voice of the pathologist. "Ahah . . ." he gave a long drawn out sigh. "I thought so."

"What, Doctor?"

With the air of a conjuror drawing a white rabbit out of an empty top hat the pathologist withdrew his hand from the rib cage, straightened up, and waved the forceps in front of Sloan. "Here's your cause of death, Inspector."

It was a bullet.

German bullets were now machine-gunning too.

7

"A bullet, Sloan?" echoed Superintendent Leeyes over the telephone.

"Yes, sir."

"A German bullet? Were they machine-gunning too, then?"

Sloan cleared his throat. "A British bullet, sir."

There was a pause. Then.

"I see, Sloan. Not death by action of the King's enemies after all."

"No, sir, I'm afraid not. Not the—er—common enemy at all, sir, but a personal one, I should say. Dr. Dabbe thinks the point of entry was the upper aspect of the fifth left rib."

Leeyes grunted down the line. "Trying for the heart."

"It lodged in the spinal vertebrae anyway, sir. That's where Dr. Dabbe found it."

"This bullet . . ."

"A .303, sir."

"Ha! That's a good clue, Sloan."

"Is it, sir?"

"Dad's Army."

"Pardon, sir?"

"Dad's Army, Sloan."

"That's what I thought you said, sir. What," asked Sloan cautiously, "was Dad's Army?"

"Don't you remember, Sloan?"

"No, sir."

"What did you do in the war then?"

"Went to school, sir."

"What? Good Lord, Sloan, are you as young as all that?"

"Not as young as all that," murmured Sloan demurely, "but not old enough to know about Dad's Army."

"The Home Guard, man. In case of invasion. The people who came after the Local Defence Volunteers. L.D.V.'s they were known as at first." He chuckled sardonically. "The Look, Duck, and Vanish brigade we called them at the time."

"Really, sir?" That must have been a great encouragement.

"The Home Guard had .303s to begin with. They had some Canadian issue rifles later but it was .303s first."

Sloan wrote that down. Dr. Dabbe had promised him a full report on the bullet as soon as possible but all information was grist to a good detective's mill.

"After the pikes and pitchforks," said Leeyes reminiscently. "You'd be surprised how many pillars of society reckoned they could take someone with them when they went."

"Really, sir?"

"Gentle old ladies talking fit to make your blood run cold. It'll be different next time." He grunted. "What else have you discovered?"

"The skeleton was recovered from the cellar of a bombed house occupied by some people called Waite and later sold to a man, Gilbert Hodge. I'm on my way to see him now. It had been buried roughly the same length of time as the house has been bombed . . ."

"You're getting pedantic, Sloan."

"Yes, sir." Sloan went sturdily on. "Neither son of the house was married at the time of the bombing though both were of marriageable age then . . ."

"Were they?"

"There were no daughters. The woman could have been another relative or a friend . . ."

"Very friendly she must have been, Sloan, seeing as how you said she was pregnant . . ."

"Or she might have had no connection with the Waite family at all and been buried in the ruins later."

"Just good friends, Sloan," declared Leeyes. "That's what you'll find it will have been. It always is."

"I couldn't begin to say, sir," said Sloan austerely. "Not at this stage."

"Well," said Leeyes irritably, "you'd better find out . . ."

"I'm afraid there's something else, sir," said Sloan, and told him about the Museum Curator's pegs having been moved.

The response was immediate.

"Are you trying to tell me, Sloan," roared the superintendent down the telephone from the police station, "That there's still some monkey business going on on that site now?"

"I don't really know, sir, yet," admitted Sloan unhappily. He had barely taken in what the pathologist had said before the implications of the archeologist's moved pegs started to hit him.

"Well, why haven't you . . ."

"I've only been able so far to have a word with this young chap Colin Rigden on the telephone at his work." The pathology laboratory telephone wasn't the most convenient one in the world either: though there was no use saying so to the superintendent. If your eyes so much as strayed from the telephone they saw something very nasty in a bottle. Pickled.

"Well?"

"He swears the dig was all pegged out for him when he got to Lamb Lane early on Saturday morning with his friends—just like Mr. Fowkes had said it would be."

"But away from this wall you were talking about?"

"Yes, sir."

"And the Museum man says he left it all pegged out near the wall?"

"That's right, sir."

"On the Friday afternoon . . ."

"Yes, sir. He and his caretaker got back to the Museum about four o'clock. And then he went off to London."

"Confirmed?"

"Not yet, sir." Sloan took a breath. "So no wonder this Rigden fellow didn't find any late Saxon remains . . ."

"And no wonder," snarled Superintendent Leeyes nastily, "that he didn't find any late English ones either."

"No, sir."

"You realise what this means, Sloan?"

"Yes, sir."

"That somebody knew this skeleton was there and didn't want it found."

"Somebody around now."

"Exactly." Leeyes grunted. "Blows the case right open again, doesn't it . . ."

"Narrows it a bit, too," pointed out Sloan, "to those people who knew about Fowkes and his pegs and who were free late Friday night or early Saturday morning to do a bit of alteration work."

"There's your next move then," said Leeyes. "Find out who moved the pegs and why and you're more than halfway there."

"Yes, sir." Detection in two easy lessons?

"Someone," pronounced the superintendent pontifically, "has obviously been taking a keen interest in this particular development." Suddenly his voice changed. "Good God, Sloan . . ."

"What, sir?" urgently.

"Dick's Dive . . ."

"What about it?"

"There's a man—a man, mark you, Sloan—just come out with a necklace on and . . ." the superintendent choked, "he's carrying a ladies' handbag."

Inspector Sloan telephoned Mark Reddley and Associates (Developers) Ltd from the pathology laboratory too.

He was put through by an efficient switchboard girl who unobtrusively held him at bay while she established who Sloan was.

"Mr. Reddley's just coming on the line now, sir . . ."

"Inspector?" That was Reddley's voice now. Swift and economical without being abrupt.

Sloan said, "I'm very sorry, sir, but I'm afraid I can't give you the go-ahead in Lamb Lane just yet after all."

"Why not?"

"We haven't completed our investigations into the site." Formulae did have their uses sometimes. He was aware of an impatient sigh at the other end of the line.

"Inspector, this delay is costing a great deal of money."

"I'm sure it is, sir," he said sympathetically. "We'll be as quick as we can."

"A great deal of money," repeated Reddley. "Garton has hired machines on a daily contract basis and we have a schedule to keep."

"I can understand that, sir."

"There must be a reason for this delay . . ."

"Yes, sir, there is."

Mark Reddley waited. "Well?"

Inspector Sloan cleared his throat and changed the formula. "We're still—er—pursuing our enquiries, sir."

"You are? Then perhaps you can tell me how much longer you expect to be pursuing them at such great cost."

"No, not precisely, sir." Sloan was not a man to be stampeded. "I'm not really in a position to say at this point."

"It sounds," said Reddley savagely, "as if all I can do then, Inspector, is to wish you luck . . ."

"You could put it like that, sir," agreed Sloan meekly. "You could perhaps also help me with your memory."

"My memory?"

"We're naturally very interested in all we can learn about Lamb Lane at the time of the bombing. Were you in Berebury then?"

"Me? Oh, yes, I was here all right. I'm a Berebury man. I was at Corton's all through the war, Inspector. I worked in their drawing office . . ."

"I see, sir," said Sloan.

He did, too. It was an easy step when you came to think about it . . .

Drawing board to developer.

Rags to riches, too?

"It was a reserved occupation, of course," went on Reddley. "I kept on trying to join up but they wouldn't let me."

"I should imagine Berebury itself was pretty front line . . ."

The developer's voice sounded amused. "You can say that again, Inspector. More like a target area some nights. I think the Lamb Lane corner went in June 1941 . . ."

"That's right, sir. That would have been the Wednesday."

"But I must say I hadn't realised that there was anyone missing from there at the time."

"I don't think anyone had, sir," said Sloan mendaciously.

Someone had known perfectly well.

He knew that now.

"Usually," said Reddley, "there was quite a hue and cry, you know, if the Rescue people thought there was anyone still buried . . ."

"I'm sure there was, sir." Sloan didn't say quite how well buried the woman had been.

"But the Wednesday was just about the worst raid of the lot," said Reddley. "That was the same night they got Corton's workshop."

"Was it?"

"They'd been trying to get it for weeks, as I remember. People said they were after the houses but we knew better. It was Corton's they wanted and in the end it was Corton's they got. Took two days to get the fire out . . ."

"Did it, sir?" said Sloan.

"We started off," said Reddley neatly, "by firewatching for fires but I'm afraid we ended up by just watching one big fire."

Sloan got Gilbert Hodge's address from the sergeant on duty at the police station.

"Number 19, Glebe Street, St. Luke's, sir."

"Nothing known?"

"Not officially, sir, yet for all that he's made a mint of money . . ."

"Don't be cynical, Sergeant."

"No, sir. Sorry, sir. I'm told he started from nothing and climbed up."

70

"There's nothing wrong in that. What's his line?"

"Buying cheap and selling dear," retorted the sergeant, "though," he added thoughtfully, "I'd say not all his deals were as simple as that."

"Clever," decided Sloan, putting down the telephone. He did not mean it as a compliment.

Gilbert Hodge gave Detective Inspector Sloan and Detective Constable Crosby an equally cautious reception.

They found him in his builders' merchant's yard in his shirt sleeves. The shirt was not conspicuously clean: his fingernails were positively dirty. Two deeply ingrained lines ran from the corners of his mouth down into his chin. The rest of his face was pointed; sharp.

Somewhere not very far away a railway train shunted.

Sloan told him about the skeleton. "I expect you've heard already."

He nodded. "Garton told me. He was round here."

"We understand you own the site . . ."

"I do now. I didn't before. Bought it off Harold Waite when he decided to sling his hook."

"Why?"

Hodge shrugged his shoulders. "Corner site. Bound to improve in value. Did a fair bit of that sort of buying at the time. People wanted to sell then."

"You've had a long wait."

Hodge grinned. His teeth weren't very good. "Haven't lost, Inspector."

"The rest of the site . . ."

Hodge grinned again. "Mine. Bought it up as it came on the market. It's going to look nice. Reddley's made a good job of the plans. Did them himself. Shops with offices on top. Unusual design though. Didn't like it meself."

"Oh?"

"Not my choice. Reddley's. He did something really fancy before but the Council wouldn't wear it."

"Really?" Sloan made a note of that.

Hodge jerked his shoulder. "Though don't ask me what that lot know about design."

"No . . ."

71

"Anyway Reddley says you've got to keep up to date these days and he should know what he's talking about."

Sloan nodded. Up to date meant concrete and glass and twiddly bits.

"But none of this here sculpture," declared Hodge. "He wanted to put something on the wall. Symbolic, he called it."

"Did he?" Symbolic wasn't a word that the police had a lot of use for. It was too popular with other people for that. People like psychiatrists and demonstrators.

"I told him," said Hodge, "I wasn't having fancy bits of old iron dressed up as art. I'm old-fashioned meself."

"Yes . . ."

"The scrap yard's the place for that." He shrugged. "Still, the design can't be too bad. Three of the places are let already."

Sloan nodded again. The proof of the commercial pudding was always in the eating—which made for a certain simplicity.

"This skeleton . . ." he said.

Hodge cocked his head to one side. "That's Garton's worry, Inspector. Not mine. He's building the place."

"It's my worry, too," said Sloan firmly, "and nobody's building anything until I've sorted it out."

Hodge waved a hand. "I shan't press Garton . . ."

"He gets his stuff through you . . ."

Hodge bared his teeth again in a semblance of a smile. "Well, now, Inspector, you wouldn't expect him to get it from anyone else, would you?"

"No, Mr. Hodge, I don't know that I would."

"And it's in the contract to make sure," said Hodge with satisfaction. "Never was one for gentlemen's agreements meself."

"No . . ." Sloan wouldn't have expected him to have been. You didn't get rich that way.

"That doesn't mean to say," said Hodge cheerfully, "that Reddley isn't pressing him. If he's got three tenants already I expect he is."

Sloan began to get a glimmer of why Garton seemed so anxious to please. He was caught between Reddley

72

and Hodge for a start. He hoped he knew what he was doing because for Sloan's money both of the other two did.

"The Waite boys," he said. "I suppose you know them too?"

"Lord, yes," said Hodge. "We were all youngsters round here together. Harold was always stuffy but Leslie . . ." He leered at Sloan. "Leslie was a right lad."

"We're on our way to see him now."

8

"All missing persons, sir?"

"That's what I said."

"Since 1941?"

"Since 1941," said Sloan grimly. He'd got to start his routine somewhere and the bombing of the house was as good a beginning as any other.

He was talking to an elderly, dyspeptic and very, very slow constable in the Records Department of Berebury Police Station who was known as Lightning Brown while Detective Constable Crosby went in search of Leslie Waite's present address.

"It'll take a bit of time, sir," said Lightning.

"I daresay," said Sloan pleasantly.

"Had one last Friday night. A girl last seen thumbing a lift from a lorry on the London Road."

"Not her."

"Bank Holiday we had one that had had a row with her dad about coming home late. Hasn't been seen since."

"Before then," said Sloan evenly.

P.C. Lightning Brown started flicking through a file. Sloan didn't think he could have done it more slowly if he'd tried.

"Last November, sir, there was the Treasurer of Corton's Christmas Club."

"What happened to him?" asked Sloan in spite of himself.

"Don't rightly know, sir, but we found his clothes and a note on the cliffs above Kinnisport." He sucked his lips expressively. "Funny how they always take their clothes off, isn't it?"

"Very."

"In 1949," said Lightning Brown in measured tones, "there was one of our dentists. Walked out one night and was never seen again."

"Dull work, dentistry. Nothing but teeth all day." Sloan thought of the dental picture that the pathologist would have waiting for him by now. Perhaps that would be a quicker way to a name than this.

"He wasn't the only one that night," volunteered Lightning.

"No?"

"His girl went too."

"His girl?"

The man scowled. "Chairside assistants they call themselves nowadays."

"Quite." Somehow Sloan didn't think the skeleton in Lamb Lane, however pregnant, was the dentist's chairside assistant but he would have to make sure. He took down the details. It would have been a different story if the dentist hadn't gone too.

Quite a different story.

He would have been much more interested then in the chairside assistant missing since 1949. As Sloan saw it the bullet and the burial meant that someone wanted to stay.

Not go.

Wanted to stay badly enough to kill the lady in question before her baby was born and wanted to bury her so that nobody knew about either body or baby.

Therefore someone who had a stake in being in Berebury?

"Go on going back," he commanded Lightning Brown.

"Two more hitches on the London Road. If only," he said in a grumbling way, "they'd write. Save us a lot of bother."

They never did.

Sloan knew that.

Whatever it was drove them away stopped them writing too. And those who were left at home could never see that. It was just those ties—or apron strings—or tentacles—that they wanted to break with in the first place. And having broken them didn't want to join them neatly together again with the knot of a letter or an address.

"Come home. All forgiven. Mum and Dad," murmured Sloan.

"Fido pining," said the old constable cynically. "That'd bring 'em back quicker. Of course, there's not a lot here for some of them."

Sloan could well believe that.

The bucolic calm of an English market town wasn't every teenager's idea of the perfect adolescent environment. Not that the Lamb Lane lady had been a teenager. Dr. Dabbe had been sure about that. By the time you were twenty-three or so you had sorted out what you did want . . . you didn't want a baby, of course, if you weren't married.

Especially in an English market town.

Especially then.

Lightning grunted. "That's not what I think. That's what their solicitors say when we catch one of them for doing a spot of the old wilful damage."

"And what, may I ask, does the magistrate say to that?" enquired Sloan.

Nothing would surprise him about magistrates.

Nothing.

"Asks ever so politely if they wouldn't rather be given the church windows to smash. Must be more exciting, he says, cool like, to break coloured glass than just the plain plate glass stuff in the High Street shop windows. Keen on damages, he is."

"I'm glad to hear it," said Sloan. Though where damages got you with the Dick's Dive mob he wouldn't know. If they didn't believe in wealth then fines were scarcely punishment. Possessing nothing which normal society valued made threatening to take it away so much hot air.

Trying to explain this to the superintendent had been wasted breath, too.

The disgruntled constable went back to his old files. "Then there was the war. You interested in the war, sir?"

"Yes," said Sloan for the first time in his life.

"There were the deserters, of course. Always one or

two of them making for home comforts. Premature de-mobilisation with some of 'em. Wanted to get back."

"And civilians missing after air raids?"

The constable shook his head. "Nobody like that un-accounted for, sir. Not here in Berebury."

"Sure?"

P.C. Brown looked pained. "Dead sure, sir."

"Not even after the Wednesday?"

"No. I was here myself, sir. I remember quite well."

Sloan sighed. There were some people, of course, who were never going to get promotion. You could tell right from the start. Lightning Brown must have been one of them. Even as a young man.

"Nearest we came, sir, to a missing person or an un-identified body was a finger."

"A finger?" For a moment Sloan wondered if he was having his leg pulled.

"That's right, Inspector. I was on duty that night. The Wednesday. During the raid a chap brought his finger in to me. All done up in a napkin, it was, the wrapping of parcels not 'aving been allowed as from the fourteenth of the month."

"Nice for you."

"Very. Seems as if he'd taken it to the first-aid post near the church and they said they couldn't do nothing with it on its own so to speak."

"Quite."

"So he popped it round to the mortuary . . ."

"Did he?"

"We were using the Italian ice-cream parlour in River Street as a mortuary in those days, the bottom having fallen out of the market in a manner of speaking . . ."

"Yes?" Whoever had nicknamed Police Constable Brown "Lightning" had done a good day's work. Sloan hoped that he—whoever he was—had got promotion.

Constable Crosby came back, notebook in hand. He'd got Leslie Waite's address.

". . . Due," went on P.C. Brown unhurriedly, "to a shortage at the time of both Italians and ice cream."

"The finger," prompted Sloan.

"The mortuary wouldn't touch it without a body belonging to it. Not their pigeon, they said. So he brought it round here to the station."

"What did you do with it?" asked Sloan, fascinated in spite of his better judgement.

"Buried it beside Timoshenko out in the back yard."

"Who was Timoshenko?" inevitably.

"The station cat. She was a lady cat as it happened, but this Russian general was very popular at the time." Lightning Brown sniffed. "Next day another chap turns up and says the finger was his. He was one short naturally . . ."

"Naturally." In a minute Sloan would get up and walk out. The Ancient Mariner had nothing on P.C. Brown.

"Seems as if he was chopping wood when Moaning Minnie went and the axe slipped. He'd nipped off to the hospital before this other chap came along."

"And there was nobody else missing?"

"Nobody else, Inspector." He shut the file. "Except a young lady who wrote from a well-known address north of the Border . . ."

"I'll buy it."

"Gretna Green. I don't suppose you want to know about her."

"Just for the record." Sloan told Crosby to take down a Berebury name and address. "You never know."

"It'll have changed again," said Lightning Brown pessimistically. "That sort of marriage doesn't last."

"Sir," said Crosby as they left the Records Department, "who's Moaning Minnie?"

"A siren, Constable."

"Is she, sir?"

"A warning siren," he said swiftly. "Meaning danger overhead."

Sloan stared out of the car windows as Crosby drove out of Berebury towards Kinnisport. He had no idea what the time was. The day had somehow slipped away, unmarked by food, unpunctuated by any clock. When he was going to eat next was anybody's guess.

So was where he was going to pluck information about an old bullet in an old body.

Before as he had gone about his business in Berebury he had merely been subconsciously aware of the casual intermingling of old and new houses and shops. Today Sloan looked at them with new eyes as he realised for the first time that this randomness was the randomness of bombing.

The new buildings—the postwar buildings—suddently irritated him. They were an intrusion. He was only interested in old Berebury now. Then the police car swung away from angular unmellowed brick and overdone plate glass and out onto the main road west to Kinnisport.

Leslie Waite was obviously younger than his brother Harold. Younger and more carefree.

They ran him to earth shortly after opening time in a tiny fisherman's pub on the waterfront.

Already the little bar was crowded and noisy. "Let's try the table in the corner," Waite shouted above the hubbub. "Quieter."

He led the way across, glass in hand. The attractive youngish woman with him came too. "The wife," he said.

She smiled.

"Sit down here, Inspector," said Waite. "You did say you were an inspector, didn't you?"

"I did."

"And you've come over from Berebury to see me?"

"That's right, sir. About a strange discovery in Lamb Lane."

"Something nasty in the woodshed?"

"In the cellar, sir." Sloan looked round. The whole place was full of sailors and fishermen and their wives.

"Don't worry, Inspector. A crowd's the best place for a quiet chat." Leslie jerked his shoulder towards the bar. "Fellow over there thought he'd have a private row with his wife out in their boat. The whole mooring heard every word. Better than a play actually . . ."

"Sound does travel over open water," agreed Sloan.

"Tell me, Inspector," said Mrs. Waite, "what was in the cellar?"

Sloan told her, omitting the pregnancy and the bullet.

Leslie Waite plunged his face into his beer mug. "And you've got no shortage of bodies on the books so to speak?"

"No, sir. As it happens we haven't."

"A skeleton, eh? Well, well . . ."

"A woman's skeleton . . ."

Leslie Waite sat back on the pub bench, quite relaxed. "I was at sea when the house was bombed."

"I'll make a note of that "

"Came home on leave to find the place a shambles. First thing I knew was when I got one of my own letters back marked Gone Away." He gave a short laugh. "It was the address that had gone away "

"Your father," said Sloan, "appears to have been quite unaware of the skeleton when he willed the house to your brother . . ."

Leslie Waite's face changed. It was no longer quite so relaxed. "You've looked that up, have you?"

"Yes, sir. A skeleton—er—requires investigation."

"Harold was always the white-haired boy. I was always the black sheep." He swept up the glasses from the table. "Quite sure you're not drinking, Inspector?"

"Quite sure, sir, thank you," said Sloan.

Crosby said nothing.

"I'm afraid I sowed a few wild oats too many for the old man."

"I see, sir." In Sloan's opinion Hasse's rule was measuring someone's wild oat all right but he didn't know if it was Leslie Waite's or not.

Yet.

Certainly there had been no visible pricking of the ears by Leslie Waite at the mention of missing persons as there had been with Harold. But that might be because Harold had already warned him. He'd had several hours in which to do it and families were funny things. However devisive among themselves they were usually united against the police.

"He thought I was never going to make a go of anything when I came out of the Navy." Leslie pointed a thumb towards the sea. "As the only thing I wanted to do was mess about in boats perhaps the old chap was right."

There was a sudden burst of laughter from the bar. Leslie edged his way into the barman's ambit and came back with another beer.

"Do you go over to Luston much?" asked Sloan casually.

"And run the risk of conversion by my sanctimonious sister-in-law, Inspector? Not on your life!"

"Or Berebury?"

He shook his head. "No. No point in going to Berebury when you can have days like today in Kinnisport, eh, Doreen?"

"None."

"Wind right. Tide right. Heaven."

Doreen Waite smiled. "Couldn't have been better."

"You do a lot of sailing, sir?"

Leslie Waite nodded vigorously. "Every day if I can. Not like the poor Saturday and Sunday blokes."

"And the rest of the time?"

"When I'm not sailing? I work in a boat builder's yard. Unskilled. I'm not very good. Doreen's the one that keeps us going."

"Nonsense." Doreen Waite flushed. "I'm only a secretary, Inspector."

"Anyway, it's better than slaving away in a factory like old Harold. And hog-tied to a religious maniac into the bargain. He never got anywhere at all—for all that he got shot of Corton's like the others."

"What's that got to do with it?"

"His pals Reddley and Hodge did pretty well for themselves by clearing out when they did. All Harold did was change one bench for another." Leslie Waite ran his eyes lazily round the cosy little pub and put his free arm round his wife. He lifted his glass with his other arm. "But in the end I reckon I've done best of all."

"Really, sir?"

"Really, Inspector. I've got what I want without working. You can't beat that."

* * *

Detective Constable Crosby, once more behind the driving wheel, inclined his head to indicate Kinnisport fast receding behind him "If that's failure, sir, I'll have it every time, thank you very much."

"His father cut him out of his will," said Sloan.

That was a fact.

A demonstrable fact.

Demonstrable facts were a little on the short side in the case at the moment and those that existed were mostly with the pathologist.

A body.

An unborn baby.

And a bullet.

Sloan stared out of the window without seeing anything: and decided he'd got the order wrong.

An unborn baby, a bullet, and a body.

That was more like it.

The skeleton was there—on the post-mortem bench—but so far was unrelated to evidence in the police sense of that much misused word.

"Sons don't get left out of their father's wills for nothing," persisted Sloan.

If you listened to the politicians it was this obstinate determination of citizens to leave their worldly goods to their biological—not their social—heirs that caused half the taxation problems in the country.

Sloan didn't listen to the politicians, of course. He was a policeman and nearer to life as it was lived.

"That sort of failure'd suit me down to the ground." Crosby changed down a gear for a bad bend.

"Failure's a relative thing . . ." That was something else you only learnt as the years went by. Crosby wasn't old enough yet, hadn't been frustrated enough yet, hadn't been disappointed enough yet . . .

"Sails every day," said Crosby, "works with boats, nice young wife. I shouldn't mind . . ."

"In the morning," said Sloan, "you can check that she is his wife."

"Yes, sir."

"We will also check on whatever it was that made Leslie Waite a black sheep twenty-five years ago.

83

Though," he added morosely, "with the permissive society being what it is, I don't suppose it's even in the book any more." He hunched his shoulders. "Still less anyone minding."

Not with Dick's Dive clientele setting the pace.

"No, sir. Shall we," suggested Crosby sedulously, "be calling it a day now, sir?"

"No, we will not, Crosby."

"But we'll be coming to the Berebury junction in a tick, sir."

"Take the Luston Road."

"The Luston Road?"

"What we want," said Sloan flatly, "is a quiet word with Harold Waite without his wife being there."

"That's not going to be easy, sir. Don't suppose he ever nips out for a quick one. Not with a wife like that."

"You can bet your life he does," said Sloan who was older and wiser. "He couldn't manage without. Not with a wife like that."

"But must we go now, sir? After all," he added unwisely, "it's not as if it's an important job."

"Not important, Constable?"

"Not urgent then, sir," amended Crosby. "It wasn't as if all this was yesterday, is it?"

"And what," enquired Sloan majestically, "has time to do with crime?"

9

Dr. William Latimer was getting ready to leave the Feathers Hotel in Berebury. He had enjoyed his first meeting of the Caduceus Club more than he had expected he would.

The hotel itself looked as if it had come straight out of an old-fashioned Christmas card, and he had parked his car in a quaint cobbled yard built long ago for horses.

Before going inside he had straightened his tie, pulled down his waistcoat and braced himself for his first meeting with his fellow doctors—but there had been no need. The first club member he had met wasn't even wearing a waistcoat. The second looked like a prosperous farmer in from the country and the third was dressed more like a bookie than a general practitioner.

They had all been very friendly.

"You must be Latimer."

William agreed that he was.

"What are you drinking?"

This dialogue was repeated up and down the room. By the end of the evening William decided he had met almost everyone present except a lanky chap with a bow tie, who had spent the whole time at the bar deep in converse with the only lady present.

The Caduceus Club was clearly an institution for the relieving of medical feelings. William didn't take long to gather that.

"A typical appendix . . ."

"I told the Out Patient Department . . ."

"Filthy throat . . ."

"I said to Casualty . . ."

"Biggest gallstone I've ever seen . . ."

"Four late calls . . ."

"I wrote the Executive Council . . ."

"Breech . . ."

It was almost time to go before William fetched up against the lanky fellow with the bow tie who had by now said goodnight to the lady and left the bar. He shook William's hand.

"I'm Waineton. You must be Latimer."

William agreed he was.

"What are you drinking?"

William said he thought he'd had enough.

Waineton nodded in the direction of a corner table. "You're all right, old chap. The police surgeon's over there and he isn't ready to go home yet."

William changed his tactics. "Still got some, thank you," he said, waving his glass.

"Waistcoat killers," said Waineton indistinctly.

"I beg your pardon?"

"Waistcoat killers," repeated Waineton. "That's what evenings like this are. We all eat and drink too much. Everybody."

"Er—yes. You may be right."

"And how are you enjoying St. Luke's, eh?"

"I'm just settling in, you know."

"A bit difficult, of course . . ."

"Not particularly."

"Bound to be after what happened."

William looked up. "What happened?"

"You know. To old Tarde."

"I don't know."

Dr. Waineton's face changed from the convivial to the melancholy as if it was the indiarubber mask of a disappointed clown. "Poor old Tarde."

"What happened to him?" said William.

"Knew him well," muttered Waineton unsteadily. "Been in St. Luke's for years and years."

"I know that," said William, "but what happened to him?" The evening at the bar had obviously made Dr. Waineton quite maudlin.

"Didn't you know, old chap?"

"Know what?" demanded William firmly.

"I thought you'd have heard . . ."

"Heard what?"

"He committed suicide."

The Two Doves in Luston was moderately full despite the lateness of the hour.

Men in working clothes, faces none too clean, kept on slipping in through the swing doors. It wasn't a dressy pub. It was a place where a hard-working man could quench his thirst before going home through the silent streets. Silent, that is, save for the heavy throbbing of mill machinery. That never stopped.

The twilight shift, it seemed, was succeeded by the night shift proper. Men on that had presumably dropped in to slake their thirsts earlier.

Sloan and Crosby were settled at a small table in a corner, conspicuous as strangers. The rest of the clientele were clearly all known to each other and to the landlord.

There was no sign of Harold Waite.

The two policemen watched the swing doors from where they sat. This was Harold Waite's pub, all right. The man on the Bean Street beat had told them that. But though a great many men came in and out Harold Waite was not among them. Neither were any women. It got later and later.

Towards half-past the hour the landlord began to ask for the last orders.

Sloan told him he had been hoping to see Waite.

"The number two shop foreman? No"—the landlord shook his head—"he hasn't been in tonight. George! George, there's a bloke here asking for Harold Waite."

The burly fellow half-turned. "Evening, mate . . . Friend of yours, is he, then?"

"In a manner of speaking," said Sloan diplomatically. "A chap said I might find him here."

"Usually," agreed the man called George, "but he wasn't in to work this evening."

"Wasn't he?"

"Try tomorrow," advised George. "He wasn't ill or anything. Just said he had somebody to see, special like."

87

"Oh, dear . . ."

George misinterpreted Sloan's disappointed expression and said, "I expect he'll be in tomorrow, all right."

"If he's spared," said a wag standing somewhere behind him.

"Your friend," pronounced George with dignity, "has wife trouble."

"I know," said Sloan. "That's why I thought I'd have a word with him here."

This display of finer feeling on Sloan's part made an immediate appeal to George who insisted that the next round was his.

Even though the round after that was Sloan's he still could not extract from George who it was that Harold Waite had taken time off from work to go see.

He just didn't know.

A little later still a strange beep-beep started up in Dr. William Latimer's bedroom in Field House, Berebury. Dr. Latimer, pleasantly refreshed by his evening out, happened to be dreaming happily at the same time about a girl who happened to look just like Jane Appleby.

In the manner of dreams the beep-beep was instantly transmogrified into the sound of a ship's siren. The dream obligingly accommodated itself to the new noise and soon he was sailing along in a cruise liner with a girl (who happened to look just like Jane Appleby) by his side.

The beep-beep persisted. Soon it had begun to intrude on his unconscious as well as his subconscious mind.

Beep-beep.

He turned over. It couldn't be morning. There was no light sneaking round the curtains.

Beep-beep.

He was awake now. The noise was coming from beside his ear. From the old-fashioned speaking tube. He pulled out the plug and put his mouth to the tube.

"Dr. Latimer here . . ." Sleepily.

"My wife . . ." began a man's voice.

"Haven't got a wife," he said bemusedly. He would have to get one. Though a wife wasn't going to like the speaking tube. It was a real intrusion into domestic felicity. He shook himself. He wasn't married yet.

"My wife, Doctor," the disembodied voice said again. "The nurse said would you come now."

"Whose wife?"

"Mine."

"No, I mean, who are you?"

"Sorry. Tony Caldwell. You know . . ."

"I know. What exactly did the nurse say?"

"Something about five shillings, Doctor. It didn't make any sense to me."

It did to William.

"Right you are. I'll be round."

"Don't you bother about getting your car out, Doctor. I've got mine here and it'll be quicker than yours."

It was.

Much.

It was well after half-past three in the morning before the doctor turned back towards Field House and bed. He had decided to walk home.

It was a decision compounded of prudence and pleasure. Tony Caldwell had driven him to his house in a sports car of such ferocity that William had little doubt that it would have to go now that they had a baby. A young man wouldn't be able to afford both. But William had declined a lift back. It was a lovely night and it wasn't far to walk. Besides, Tony Caldwell was now in that euphoric state of first fatherhood which made his driving doubtful.

William stepped out happily, too.

This was a feeling beyond compare. A new family behind him. The pleasant, capable midwife who had been glad to meet him; the tired but happy mother; the deliriously happy father. Definitely not the chap from whom to take a lift at this moment.

He walked down past the church. Only the tower could really be said to be still standing. And a length of wall with the empty sockets of window. On the other side of the church there were only a few Saxon remains which still stood contemptuous of the Aryan blast.

The deserted bomb site looked quite sepulchral as he

walked up Lamb Lane. He spared a thought for the dead girl who had lain there all those long years.

And for Dr. Tarde.

Why had he killed himself?

He was still thinking about Dr. Tarde when he came abreast of the old bomb site.

That was when he heard something.

And had a moment's atavistic—almost animal—awareness that he was not alone.

The sound had been tiny. Stone rubbing on stone perhaps. And he couldn't place its direction very easily. It was somewhere on the site. That was all he could say. He halted in his tracks and listened intently but it did not come again.

Perhaps he had only fancied it.

Alone at half-past three in the morning it was easy to fancy something.

He swung his torch round in a wide arc across the bomb site.

He never saw what it was that hit him. The last thing he remembered was a splitting pain in his head and the terrible feeling of falling forever into a bottomless well of blackness.

The appetizing smell of frying bacon drifted out of the kitchen window of Sloan's semidetached house in Berebury. It reached him halfway down the garden path. It was another lovely September morning, and if autumn was in the offing his roses gave very little sign of it. Most of them were still in their second good flowering.

His wife, Margaret, called to him.

He went indoors slowly, reluctant to exchange the ordered beauty of his garden for the disarray of a muddled murder case with its murky motives. He said as much to his wife.

"Apt alliteration's artful aid," she retorted.

"Who said that?"

"Churchill, of course."

"Oh. Churchill." He looked at her. "Margaret, what exactly do you remember about the war?"

"The noise," she said promptly. "And not having any sweets."

With him it had been the posters.

The Ministry of Information posters. Exhorting you to do this. Or not to do that. Reducing unimaginable horrors to a series of instructions about what you should do next. Nearly all of them seemed to include reporting to the Town Hall.

That's what he was going to do today.

There had been one poster though which had shocked him. He'd seen it on a railway bridge in 1943. Coloured and clever. Something about Australia or it might have been Canada. Hinting at vast reserves of manpower and munitions ready and waiting in the wings, so to speak.

"These," had declaimed the poster, "are the sinews of war."

And what had shaken his schoolboy mind to the core had been the thought behind the propaganda.

That we had needed cheering on to victory at all.

"The blackout," his wife was saying through his reverie. "I remember that, too."

He stared blankly.

He'd forgotten all about there having been a blackout. That highly convenient darkness. He squared his shoulders. What he would have to do—and that without delay—was to fill in his background knowledge about the war. Before Superintendent Leeyes caught him out on having forgotten—or not having found out about—something dead simple.

Like the blackout.

"I'll have to go to the library today," he muttered indistinctly, speech impeded by bacon. "Do a bit of reading about the war."

"I believe they do a gramophone record, too," said Margaret Sloan, filling his cup. "A sort of instant memory reviver."

"I'm going to need more than records—of either sort—to get anywhere with this case." Sloan put down his cup and told her the whole story.

"Poor girl." She poured a cup of tea for herself and

91

sat down opposite him. "Lying there all those years without anyone knowing."

"Or caring," grunted Sloan. "That's the funny thing. She wasn't missing and I reckon she ought to have been."

"So nobody was looking for her?"

"Not that we can see."

"They must have thought she was somewhere else then . . . is that the Crosby boy at the door?"

"That's another thing that doesn't help," said her husband bitterly.

"What, dear?"

"The Crosby boy. Boy's the word. He's so young he wasn't even born when this girl was killed."

"Really, dear?"

"I daren't ask him if he knows what the war was about in case he doesn't."

"No, dear." She frowned. "But I'm not at all sure that I do either, you know. Not to put in so many words."

"Imagines it was some glorified game of Cowboys and Indians, I expect."

"Or Cops and Robbers," suggested Margaret lightly.

Sloan shook his head. "No. He'd be more interested if he thought it was them. He's got it into his head that we're investigating pre-history and that it doesn't matter anyway."

"No, dear."

The doorbell rang again.

"Let him wait," growled Sloan.

"Yes, dear," said Margaret Sloan, getting up at once and going to the door.

Detective Constable Crosby seemed to fill their dining room. He stood awkwardly to one side of Sloan's chair like a great dog waiting to be told what to do next.

"A cup of tea, William?"

"Oh, yes, thank you, Mrs. Sloan."

"You'd better sit down while you have it," said his host graciously. "Before you tread on the cat."

"Yes, sir." Crosby lowered himself gingerly onto a chair.

92

Margaret Sloan pushed some toast in front of him. He did not need a second invitaion.

"At the time of the death of the lady in Lamb Lane," said Sloan heavily, "that butter and that marmalade there would have had to do you a week."

"Would they, sir?"

"Rationing." Sloan helped himself to a liberal dollop of butter. "Surprisingly popular, I'm told it was, too— especially with the 'fair shares for all' brigade. Some people don't mind suffering as long as they don't have to do it alone."

"No, sir. That's why point duty . . ."

"Besides," said Sloan, ignoring this, "you could always let yourself go once in a while with luxuries like whale meat. And if there was an 'r' in the month you sometimes got an egg."

"More toast, William?" said Margaret. "It isn't rationed now. He didn't mean to put you off, you know."

"Thank you, Mrs. Sloan." Gratefully.

"And tea?"

"Please . . ."

"You used to get two ounces a week of tea." Margaret Sloan poured him another cup. "I always remember that because my mother told me it came to twenty-eight teaspoonfuls and you had to make it last. Sometimes I wonder how she managed, but she did. Sugar?"

"Yes, please."

"That's another thing . . ." began Sloan.

"I don't think we were any the worse for it," went on his wife serenely, "though we went without a lot." She smiled. "I shall never forget my first banana after the war . . ."

"Yes, we had no bananas," said Sloan cryptically.

"I started to peel it with a knife," said Margaret. "I'd never eaten one before, you see."

Detective Constable Crosby looked up from his second breakfast, and said seriously, "But wasn't there somewhere called the Quartermaster's Stores, Mrs. Sloan, where you could get anything?"

Sloan choked on the last slice of toast.

10

Detective Inspector Sloan had already telephoned Luston Police and now took the precaution of ringing Dr. Dabbe before he left his own home. And before he saw Superintendent Leeyes. He told the pathologist that the bomb had fallen in June 1941.

"Did it now?" said Dabbe pensively. "Well, well, well. June 1941. I was having a nice peaceful time in a prisoner of war camp by then."

"Were you, Doctor?"

"St. Válery, Inspector. That's when I got popped in the bag."

"For the whole war?"

"The whole war." Dabbe chuckled. "Never saw a woman or a child for five years. When I came out I was as bashful as a convent schoolgirl. Far too shy to talk to any woman. You'll not believe this, Sloan, but I even proposed by post."

"Pathology," divined Sloan. He'd often wondered why Dr. Dabbe had become a medical investigator.

"That's right, Inspector. The only patients you don't have to talk to." He changed his tone and went on more briskly. "Your skeleton is after the bomb. Not before. Definitely . . ."

Sloan cleared his throat. "How definitely?"

"Court of law definitely," said Dabbe. "There were bomb and broken brick fragments under her. And if she'd been buried before the bomb . . ."

"Yes?"

"She'd not have been lying as flat as she was."

Sloan could see that.

"Nevertheless," went on the pathologist, "I think whoever shot her was hopeful that the poor woman

95

would be taken as a bomb victim should she ever have been found . . ."

"Not," objected Sloan, the policeman, "with a bullet in her spine surely."

"I was coming to that," said Dabbe unhurriedly. "You see, with a .303 rifle you don't usually get a bullet staying in a body at all. You don't often get one staying in a skeleton, come to that. I reckon the clay helped there."

Sloan nodded. Roses weren't the only thing clay was good for then. He pulled his mind up with a jerk. He mustn't start thinking about his roses in the middle of a case. Not even his sturdy Queen Elizabeths . . .

"A .303 rifle's an in and out job," said Dabbe, "and there's a very good chance that in the middle of bombing raids you'd get away with . . "

"Murder," said Sloan slowly.

"Precisely. Your .303 is a high velocity weapon and at short range . . ."

"What's short range for a .303?"

"Two hundred yards."

"Two hundred yards, Doctor! You mean this woman was shot at two hundred yards?"

"At least," said Dr. Dabbe equably. "Probably rather more."

Sloan made a note.

Dabbe said, "I've arranged to have a word later this morning with a better ballistics man than I am but I'm moderately sure about the distance. Otherwise you wouldn't have found your bullet at all. Even so it might only be because she had some particularly thick clothing on at the time she was shot."

"It might have been winter," agreed Sloan. "We don't know yet."

"Or evening."

"A leather coat," suggested Sloan. "She might have been wearing a leather coat. They're pretty stout things, you know."

"Except, Inspector," the other reminded him neatly, "that women didn't wear them at the time. Not leather coats. They weren't in fashion then. People just had utility clothes."

As he replaced the telephone receiver Sloan decided that the Public Library would have to have first priority.

Before he made a really serious mistake over the differences between then and now.

In the police car he told Crosby the gist of what the pathologist had said.

"Two hundred yards!" echoed that worthy, just as Sloan himself had done. "That's not exactly 'waiting until you can see the whites of their eyes' sort of stuff, sir, is it?"

"No." Sloan fidgeted unhappily in the front passenger seat. "Not like you and pedestrains, Constable. Look out—you nearly had that woman there . . ."

Crosby swerved obediently.

"And I suppose, sir," he said as soon as they were back on course, "just to make it more fun for us everyone had a rifle at the time?"

"Almost," agreed Sloan glumly. He couldn't see this case ever getting started—let alone finishing. "After Dunkirk all servicemen took their weapons home on leave with them. And the Home Guard had theirs all the time."

Crosby slid through some traffic lights on the amber.

"That bit about fighting on the beaches and in the streets, then, they meant it, did they, sir?"

"They did."

"Of course, next time," said that child of the present, "there won't be any fighting, will there, sir?"

"Oh, and why not?"

"We'll all be incinerated," said Detective Constable Crosby cheerfully, "in the first five minutes."

Luston might not be the most picturesque of English towns but their police force was nothing if not on the ball.

Sloan had barely got to his own desk at Berebury Police Station before there was a bright sergeant on the line called Pritchard. He didn't sound very old.

"You rang, sir, about a Harold Waite . . ."

"I haven't forgotten, Sergeant," said Sloan evenly. In

fact, Harold Waite hadn't been out of his thoughts all morning.

Harold Waite, who had left Berebury after the war because he couldn't settle down again in his own home town.

Harold Waite, who had stood still in his working career while his erstwhile friends and colleagues had gone on to better things.

Harold Waite, in whose mind the mention of the missing girl had definitely rung a bell.

"Well?" barked Sloan.

"His wife says he's missing."

Sloan groaned aloud.

"I beg your pardon, sir?" Sergeant Pritchard's anxious voice came down the line. "I didn't quite catch what you . . ."

Most important of all, Harold Waite who had now disappeared.

"Nothing. Go on."

"Seems as if he didn't come home last night after the twilight shift at his factory . . ."

"How do you know?" He didn't doubt the man. It was just that after a while it became automatic, this checking on facts. Then—and not before then—you could be said to have the true police mind.

"Bed not slept in, sir. And supper not eaten." Sergeant Pritchard coughed. "I gather Mrs. W. wasn't one of those who waited up. Just left him something in the oven. This morning when she came down . . ."

"Supper still in oven," said Sloan flatly. "What else did she say?"

"Praise not the day before evening," said Pritchard uneasily. "That's all she said."

He put down the telephone and went in to make his report to Superintendent Leeyes. The superintendent was standing at his window staring down at the Market Square.

"They're getting worse, Sloan," he said excitedly. "Look at that one. There. Now, you tell me. Is that a boy or a girl?"

Sloan followed his gaze to the youthful figure lounging on the pavement outside Dick's Dive, took in the long hair, the trousers and the sexless, epicene features and then averted his eyes. "I couldn't begin to say, sir, I'm sure."

"They used to say 'boys will be boys'," muttered the superintendent, "but . . ."

"Yes, sir."

"I don't know what we're coming to . . ."

"No, sir. About . . ."

"Ah, yes, how is the case of Yorick's lady friend?"

"I beg your pardon, sir . . . oh, I see. Yorick's lady friend, of course. We've made a start but I'm not happy about Harold Waite."

"That's the one married to the Bible puncher?"

"Yes, sir."

"Not likely to overlook a little peccadillo like getting a girl friend into trouble. . . "

"No, sir, but . . ."

"Well then," said Leeyes largely, "you're halfway there, aren't you?" He swung back towards the window. "Look, Sloan, there's another of them. They ought to be run in for personation, that's what should happen to them."

"Yes, sir." Sloan took a step back. Perhaps he could get away now. "We're just going round to the Public Library . . ."

"The Public Library, Sloan? Good God, what on earth do you want to go to the Public Library for?"

"The war, sir," explained Sloan patiently. "I feel I must get hold of some background stuff seeing how that's when the skeleton dates from. Put everything into perspective a bit, I hoped."

"Perspective? What you should be doing is finding out who killed her and," as a distinct afterthought, "who she was anyway."

"Yes, sir, I know but it was all so long ago and I'm afraid I don't remember myself what . . ."

"Some things were different," agreed the superintendent loftily. "There were guns all over the course. And I must say the greens weren't as well kept as they should have been."

"The greens, sir?"

"The greens. On the golf course. The rough went very early on. Splendid fodder it made, too, I'm told. That was a good thing."

"Was it, sir?" Sloan didn't play golf.

"Well, it wasn't when it came back after the war because, of course, you'd got used to it not being there."

"Quite," said Sloan noncommittally.

"And we had sheep on the fairways. After all, as the Committee said, there was a war on."

"Quite," said Sloan again.

"You had to pick up all the bomb and shell splinters you could on the way round to save the mowing machine."

"As well as replacing the divots?" That much he did know.

"And the Rules had to be changed." The superintendent was getting well into his stride now. "You could take cover in a competition without penalty for ceasing play during gunfire and while bombs were falling, you know."

Sloan cleared his throat. "That seems—er—quite reasonable, sir."

Or was it a case of "England expects that every golfer . . ."?

"It wasn't all in your favour like that," grunted Leeyes. "If a bomb exploding put you off your shot there was a penalty. You lost a stroke."

"Not your head?" muttered Sloan wildly.

"Damned illogical, if you ask me. Losing a stroke because of a blasted bomb."

"Did it happen often, sir?"

"Often enough," growled the superintendent. "Ruddy great high explosive came down on the twelfth one day . . ."

"That crater would have taken a bit of filling in . . ."

"Filling in!" he snorted. "The Committee didn't fill it in. They tidied up the edges, put some sand in the bottom and called it a bunker. But it wasn't the ones that went off that were the trouble. It was the others. The unexploded ones."

100

Sloan tried his best to sound sympathetic. "I can imagine that."

"There was a delayed action bomb on the approach to the ninth . . . they marked it with a red flag. Took four days to go off."

"Another bunker, sir?"

"A water hazard, Sloan. Devilish position for it. I can't tell you the number of times I've been in there since. Couldn't be in a worse place if the Committee had put it there themselves. Efficient fellows, those Germans, I will say that for them."

The lady in Lamb Lane was a sort of delayed action affair too—just exploded—when you came to think of it.

Without the red flag.

Sloan said as much to the superintendent.

"They," pronounced Leeyes ominously, "were always the most trouble in the long run." He grunted. "And it's not all quiet on the Western front either. Your friend, Dr. Latimer, was clobbered in the night. Down by that precious site."

Sloan cocked his head. "Oh?"

"Watch and wallet job. Won't be able to count any pulses until he gets another."

The surgical dressing which had been put on Dr. Latimer's lacerated scalp had one unexpected result.

At his morning surgery.

It brought about a subtle change in that delicate human situation known throughout the world as the doctor-patient relationship.

The balance of power was marginally altered: the ordering of positions was not what it was.

There was a minuscule retreat on William Latimer's part from the normal Buddha-like attitude adopted by all doctors as the fountainhead of medical wisdom. Fountainheads of wisdom did not normally have bandaged heads.

There was a fractional advance by the patients. Sympathy was tendered.

And accepted.

101

He took his morning surgery as he did all his work, slowly. This was not only because his head was still sore but because he was still feeling his way with people whose case and family histories were new to him. Dr. Tarde, of course, would have been able to have gone more quickly because he knew them all. As nobody seemed to tire of telling him, Dr. Tarde had known everything and everybody in St. Luke's.

And he had committed suicide.

"Miss Tyrell . . ."

"Yes, Doctor?"

"If you ever catch me prescribing aspirin for a really bad headache will you remind me about today?"

"Yes, Doctor."

"It's no good. No good at all."

"No, Doctor."

"Just a placebo." Latimer put an exploratory hand up in the direction of a lump on his scalp that seemed—from the inside anyway—to be about the size of Everest. "I'd no idea you couldn't walk through the streets here at night without getting hit on the head."

Miss Tyrell said that there were some very funny people about these days and asked if he had been hurt anywhere else.

"No." William started to shake his head in a traditionally negative manner and then thought better of it. It hurt less if he kept it still. "But it's enough."

"You look a little better now than you did first thing," said Miss Tyrell judiciously.

"I feel a little better. Not that I got a lot of sleep. By the time the police had been all over the place there wasn't a lot of night left." He pressed a buzzer. "Who's next?"

It was a fat, garrulous woman called Mrs. Lepton.

"Me, again, Doctor," she said, flopping down into the chair and panting slightly. "Me legs. Giving me gyp, the left one is. Lepton had to make me a cup of tea at three o'clock this morning. Couldn't sleep with it. Not a wink."

William stripped off the discoloured bandage and murmured something about her overweight not helping.

102

"I don't eat enough to keep a bird alive," she retorted smartly. "I don't know where it all comes from I'm sure."

"Keeping the legs elevated would help, too," he said, "Give it a better chance of healing."

"Oh, I couldn't keep it up," she said promptly. "I've got Lepton to see to. And the house and everything."

"It isn't going to get better if you don't." William laid fresh strips of tulle dressing across Mrs. Lepton's leg and diverted her by asking what Dr. Tarde had done for it in the past.

"Same as you, Doctor. But it never got any better. Me mother had bad legs, too. Ow . . ."

"Sorry," said William. He could see that Mrs. Lepton's left leg was going to be on the winning side in an unequal struggle between Nature and Heredity on the one hand and Medicine on the other. "You must have seen quite a lot of Dr. Tarde with a leg like this."

"Twice a week," she said with satisfaction, "until the end. He looked at it on his very last day. You'd never have known, Doctor, what he was going to do. Never. I was his last patient that morning—I usually wait until the end so as I don't keep anyone waiting—'cept Gilbert Hodge. I told Gilbert to go in afore me but he wouldn't." She sniffed. "Liked using the free chairs, I expect . . . No, that night Dr. Tarde . . ."

If Miss Tyrell's brief knock could conceivably have come after—not before—her entry into the consulting room, William would have sworn that was the way it was.

When Mrs. Lepton had gone William said quietly, "I know about Dr. Tarde, Miss Tyrell. Somebody told me last night."

"I thought they would," she said bitterly.

"I was bound to hear . . ."

Her gaunt features were as still as carved stone. "Putting you in the picture, they'd call it."

"Why did he do it?"

"I don't know. That's the terrible part. I just don't know." She turned her face away from him but he had already seen the blank mask of misery there. "He didn't tell me, Doctor. And I used to think he told me everything."

As gently as he could he asked how Dr. Tarde had done it.

Her face was bleak. "He hanged himself."

11

War, it seemed, was a subsection of history.

Bombing came under Air History.

The Bombing of England came before the Bombing of Germany but that was alphabetical.

"See also," ran the catalogue, "Art, Destruction of."

When the two policemen found the bookshelves they discovered that there was not so much as a book about the bombing of England as a whole literature.

They had gone to the Public Library after Sloan had put out a general call for Harold Waite and Crosby had sent a list of names to the General Register Office at Somerset House.

Now Detective Constable Crosby was surveying the serried rows of books. "You mean, sir, they wrote all that about it?"

Sloan followed his gaze. " 'Twas a famous victory."

"Beg pardon, sir?"

"Nothing, Crosby." Sloan pulled out a book at random. This was going to be much more difficult than he had thought. There were so many books.

Crosby cleared his throat and read aloud. "An Anderson shelter is made of heavy galvanised cast iron . . ."

"Here we are." Sloan put out his hand for a book. "This is the one we want. *Calleshire at War: A History.* I expect this will tell us what we want to know . . ."

It didn't really.

It recorded that there had been 2522 alerts, 239 incidents, 1364 High Explosive Bombs, 6 oil bombs, 18,300 incendiaries (approx.) 13 flying bombs, 27 shells (enemy), 20 crashed enemy aircraft, 9 machine gun and cannon fire incidents and 12 mines (parachute) in the town itself.

Then it went on to describe the legal structure of the county under fire. Sloan got confused about the Clerk of the Peace and the Clerk of the War Zone Court being one and the same person and put the book back.

"They had a bomb called a Bouncing Billy," remarked Crosby whose Christian name was William.

But by then Sloan had got on to the books the American correspondents had written about England in wartime.

Nobody could have called them Isolationists.

"I see," wrote one of the very best, "that in the middle of a war you still grow marigolds."

The same writer had noted that before the Fall of France the grass in the Tuileries had not been cut . . .

"I asked a policeman this morning," wrote somebody else, "did he expect invasion? He smiled broadly and said 'Not *really*,' as though I had enquired if he believed in fairies."

Sloan looked to see what Churchill had to say.

"They had no firsthand knowledge of defeat and, being a remarkably unimaginative people, have never been able to conceive of it as more than a theoretical possiblity."

He put the book back.

Four minutes' warning. Wasn't that what you were supposed to have nowadays? Before somebody—on one side or the other—or both—used weapons that weren't very nice. The weapons with the ominous name of Ultimate. Where the outcome was likely to be nonsurvivable.

Constable Crosby had stumbled on another school of authorship.

"These people, sir, seemed to think it was all political."

"Everything's political," said Sloan.

"No, I mean that they're saying that it was the Government's fault and the Council's fault—not the enemy's."

"Some people," began Sloan, "will always . . ."

106

"They say that they should have had shelters earlier," read Crosby, "and better facilities . . ."

"And more money," supplied Sloan.

"That's right, sir. How did you know?"

"Because they're the 'If you take away from me what you haven't got, and then we'll be equal brigade,' that's why," said Sloan. "Spot 'em anywhere, any time."

But Crosby had already gone on to something else.

"Sir, do you know how they worked out their casualties?"

"Counted them?" suggested Sloan.

"Standardised Killed Rate per Ton," said Constable Crosby upon whom sarcasm in any shape or form was quite wasted.

"You don't say." The book Sloan had open now was comparing bombed London with Pompeii. Most of them did that. Craters, debris, blackened rubbish, and a few charred walls . . .

In the end they got the most practical information out of *Air Raid Precautions—An Album containing a Series of Cigarette Cards of National Importance. Price One Penny.*

It was after that that Detective Constable Crosby set out to visit every dental surgery in the city.

And to chat up every dental receptionist in sight.

Some of them were formal and businesslike. Some of them giggled. None of them was old. They were all helpful.

No less than three of them were altogether too helpful. They started off on quite the wrong tack. They thought he'd come about making an appointment for filling the cavity in his eyetooth.

Crosby, who didn't like to hear what he thought of as a small hole described as a cavity, disabused them quickly.

What he had come about, he said to them all, was an old patient. The police, he said, knew her teeth but not her name.

A little matter of identification.

Before their time, of course.

About twenty-five years ago.

Dusty, yellowing records, their edges curling up, came out of all sorts of unlikely places. He was required to stand on chairs to reach the top of old cupboards, to crawl into odd holes under staircases and—in one case—to scramble up into a loft.

In between various distractions and extractions a series of very pretty girls flipped over what he had retrieved, comparing their records with Dr. Dabbe's report.

None of the records tallied with the teeth of the lady in Lamb Lane.

They were uniformly regretful that they hadn't been able to be of more assistance to—er—Detective Constable . . . er . . .

Crosby.

But if they could help him in any other way at any time he wasn't to hesitate to let them know. Now, about his eyetooth . . .

Crosby fled.

He went to a part of the town that the guide books didn't mention. The only medieval touch about this area of the town was the nearness of each house to its neighbour—touching on either side and nearly touching fore and aft. The ease with which people could converse across the street from their doorsteps was simply demonstrated by the fact that two women were doing so when he arrived.

He would have steered the police car into Aspen Close but espied difficulties in getting it out again. True, there was a banjo turning at the far end but one half of this was already occupied by an old car. It looked as if it had been there for a very long time and—unless given considerable mechanical aid—was going to go on staying there. A child's tricycle had been abandoned in the middle of the road.

He walked down to number seventeen.

"It's no use your knocking on that door, young man," said one of the conversing women. "She's next door with Mrs. Smith and the old lady's as deaf as a post."

"Thank you."

"And diddle-o with it," supplemented the woman from across the road. "So if she does hear you, you still don't get any sense out of her. You try next door. She's just got back from doing her offices. She'll be having a cup of tea with Mrs. Smith."

Crosby obediently knocked on the door of number nineteen.

It opened with the speed of light. He was conscious of a head covered in curlers and the flash of equally ferocious teeth. "If you've come about the instalments on the motor bike . . ."

"I haven't," said Crosby with dignity. "I want a word with a Mrs. Murgatroyd."

"The old lady? You won't get a sensible word out of her, young fellow." The ferocious teeth snapped open and the curlers rippled like jelly as their owner shouted, "Hilda! Hilda! There's a man here wants to see your mother."

A tired-looking woman came hurrying through from the back. "Is he from the Welfare?"

"No," said Crosby a trifle distantly.

"You'd better come in home," said the woman called Hilda, looking him up and down. She led the way in to number seventeen, carefully shutting the door against the neighbours before she said, "Well, what is it?"

She leant back against the hall wall as she spoke as if to cushion herself against what he had to say.

"I'm from the police."

The lines on the woman's face sunk in more deeply, and her mouth tightened. Even Crosby was experienced enough to know that they could not have been totally unfamiliar words.

"What is it this time?" she said. "Which one is it and what have they done?"

"It's not that." He felt clumsy. "We're just making a few enquiries about a young girl who Mrs. Murgatroyd reported as missing from this address in 1942 . . ."

"That was me," said the woman tonelessly.

"Hilda Murgatroyd? But . . ." Crosby floundered. The woman he was looking at now could have passed for sixty.

Easily.

"Hilda Murgatroyd that was. Hilda Marshall now, if you must know. What's it all about, eh?"

"We just wanted to make sure you were alive. Someone's been found . . ."

"Huh." Mrs. Marshall gave a bitter laugh. "If you can call it living."

"You ran away to Gretna Green . . ."

"Daftest thing I ever did," she said. "Talk about love's young dream."

"You came back?"

"Of course I came back. Back to everything I ran away from. There wasn't anywhere else to go. He hadn't got anywhere to take me."

"I see."

"Married woman that I was," she went on, "me dad belted me and here I am now looking after me mother who's out of her mind, and six kids and all their problems." She looked at Crosby with the grand tolerance of the old for the young, "and, in case you don't like to ask, love's young dream . . ."

"Mr. Marshall . . ."

"Mr. Marshall"—she invested the name with curious overtones—"slipped off just after our youngest was born."

"I see," said Crosby uneasily.

"Kept on calling him Tail End Charlie, he did," she said, "and I think he wanted to make sure. He always was afraid of responsibility. That was his trouble."

Dr. William Latimer stirred his coffee, took another aspirin and reflected that lines of thought exhibited just as many rules of behaviour as did their mathematical counterparts.

It was just that they did not behave with the same precision.

Miss Tyrell's train of thought was showing every sign of Newton's First Law of Motion—moving forever in a straight line until deflected. The straight line led to Dr. Tarde.

"Doctor . . ."

"Yes?"

"If anyone—any of the patients, I mean,—should ever give you any sort of hint that they knew what made Dr. Tarde do it"—she twisted and untwisted her bony fingers—"would you tell me?"

"Certainly." He hesitated. "You've no idea yourself?"

She shook her head.

"Doctors," he observed in a detached way, "are funny people. They tend to get odd ideas about themselves when they're ill . . . They think they're going to die when they're not. They decide everyone's conspiring to keep the truth from them. You know how it goes. They think the X-ray report's a fake and that the path lab people have been got at."

"He wasn't ill . . ."

"He may have thought he was. You can't really examine your own signs and symptoms properly, you know. And you make it worse by dashing to your own old textbooks. There's no comfort there." This was not the distillation of a lifetime's experience but another well-remembered lecture. They had been very thorough at William's medical school. "I expect he was just afraid he'd got something nasty and took the easy way out."

"No, it wasn't like that at all."

"They go to their medical friends—not necessarily in the right speciality," went on William, warming to his theme, "and ask them to tell them the worst and when they don't . . ."

"He was never ill," persisted Miss Tyrell. "Getting older, of course, but I'm sure he hadn't anything wrong with him."

"They're usually the worst when they think there is," said William. "There's no one like a neurotic for living on and on. They never die."

"That day," said Miss Tyrell flatly, "he'd been talking about his holiday and looking over his fishing tackle. His only problem that I know of was that he'd put on weight since he last wore his fishing trousers . . . and," said Miss Tyrell distantly, "I only knew that because he asked me to make an appointment for him with his tailor."

111

"Something must have disturbed him," said William.

"I know that," she agreed wearily, "but it wasn't fear of illness."

"Money?"

"He had all he needed, Doctor. Not too little—or too much, for that matter—to be a nuisance."

"And just a second cousin somewhere by way of family?"

She nodded. "He came to the funeral."

He might have been the only member of the family at the funeral, decided William privately, taking in Miss Tyrell's patent anxiety, but he certainly wasn't the only mourner.

"There was nothing," he said guardedly, "in the practice?"

"The practice, Doctor?"

"He hadn't dropped a terrible clanger with a patient? Someone young dying who shouldn't have done? You know, a mistake in diagnosis . . . or perhaps the wrong treatment?"

"No, no, there was nothing like that." She dismissed the suggestion impatiently.

"One might get ideas of atonement . . ."

"I should have known," Miss Tyrell said simply. "Besides, he would have said. He wasn't one of those doctors who think they're God or anything."

"His last day," suggested William. "Can you remember anything about it?"

"Everything," she said wretchedly. "Don't you think I haven't gone over it again and again?"

"I know he saw Mrs. Lepton and Mr. Hodge . . ."

"And about forty other people. There was nothing out of the ordinary about anyone at either surgery that day. I'm sure about that. No one was with him inordinately long either or anything like that . . ."

"His visiting list?"

"I'd thought of that, too. I've kept a copy. All just ordinary patients who were ill."

"New calls?"

"Only four. I'd thought about that, too." Miss Tyrell didn't seem to need anything to remind her who they were. "Mrs. Appleby in Park Street. She'd got gastritis.

112

A man called Collins with shingles. Old Bert Jackson with his chest and Mrs. Reddley with her old trouble . . ."

William grinned. "She's neurotic all right. Sticks out a mile."

"No children, too much money and social connections," said Miss Tyrell tersely, "but Dr. Tarde knew how to handle her."

"Letters then," suggested William. If it wasn't a patient who disturbed the balance of Dr. Tarde's mind perhaps something had come by post. "Or a telephone message?"

Miss Tyrell shook her head. "No," she said firmly, "I open the post and answer the telephone. Unless it's obviously a personal letter—but there weren't any of those that morning. I remember particularly . . ."

At that moment the surgery bell pealed through the house. Not once but again and again like some dreadful tocsin.

Miss Tyrell hurried to the door.

Gilbert Hodge was standing on the step, his hand on the bell.

"Can the doctor come over quickly, miss? To the bomb site." Hodge was so breathless he could hardly get the words out quickly enough. "There's a man there. I think he's dead."

Dr. Latimer scooped up his black bag and strode down the steps. Gilbert Hodge scurried along beside him.

"I was only taking a look round," he said defensively. "After all, I do own the place and there were no police or anybody there today so I thought I'd take a look."

"Quite." William stepped onto the rubble for the second time in search of a body. "Whereabouts?"

"The same place as the other one. I was just looking round," repeated Hodge in whom the need for speech was clearly pressing, "when I saw him. Look. There."

He looked.

In the space that until lately had been the resting place of the mortal remains of the unknown lady lay the huddled figure of a man. He was of medium build with

113

a close-cropped Army hairstyle. William got down beside him. He had asked Miss Tyrell to send for an ambulance but it was patently too late for any ambulance save for a black one without windows. He had to stoop to confirm that the man was dead—had been dead for some time now. He turned his head until he could see his pupils, noting as he did so a small hedge-tear scar which ran down the corner of his left forehead.

"Anyone know who he is?"

Gilbert Hodge stirred at his side. "I know him, Doctor," he said thickly. His own colour had turned quite green. "I know who that is all right though I haven't seen him in years. He's called Harold Waite."

12

While Crosby interviewed the dental receptionists, Sloan made for the local Planning Department offices. The man he saw there was as helpful as all the dental receptionists had been—but much more positive too.

"Lamb Lane?" The planning officer grinned cheerfully. "One of the biggest files we've got here."

"Really?"

"Only one factor missing over the years."

"What was that?"

"The preservationists." The man rolled his eyes expressively. "Once they get the bit between their teeth I can tell you . . ."

"There's nothing to preserve in Lamb Lane," said Sloan. Hitler had seen to that. It was rather the reverse, if anything. An eyesore.

The man gave a short laugh. "You don't suppose they'd let a little thing like that put them off, do you, Inspector?"

"Like that, are they?"

"Some of them. If they had a mind to, I daresay it wouldn't take them long to find a peg to hang something on." He twisted his lips. "Like saying the area was rich in German associations."

Sloan thought for a moment, entering into the spirit of the thing. " 'An increasingly rare memento of historic and stirring times'."

The man grinned. "That's the idea. They haven't tried it on Lamb Lane yet but you never know." He opened the file. "Whereabouts do you want to begin?"

"The beginning."

"That would be before the war. There was a bit of

115

talk about slum clearance that way but it didn't come to anything. Then we got the clearance done for us by the bomb in a manner of speaking."

"So they weren't beautiful, those houses . . ."

"Calleshire vernacular architecture," said the planner. "Good of their kind." He turned a page. "After the bombing the Council slapped a specified area notice on it pursuant to Section 7 (2) of the War Damage Act 1941."

Sloan struggled to write down the far from Plain Words. "Would that mean anything?"

"I'll say," responded the planner vigorously. "If you want chapter and verse . . ." He changed his tone to a chant and recited: "This course would prohibit any person making good war damage (other than temporary works) to hereditaments in the specified area, and would impose on such persons an obligation to inform the War Damage Commission of any proposed works."

Sloan sat up. "Then why did Gilbert Hodge buy it?"

"Search me," said the man equably. "Running a high risk of a C.P.O."

"That wouldn't be a Chief Petty Officer, by any chance, would it?"

"Sorry. Compulsory Purchase Order to the uninitiated. Nasty things, C.P.O.s, Inspector. Don't ever let one of them get you. Brings on apoplexy quicker than anything I know."

"And did they have one of those in Lamb Lane?"

"Nearly. Very nearly. Earlier this year." He ruffled through the pages. "Looks as if they had no end of schemes for this and that after the war . . ."

"Homes fit for heroes anyway," said Sloan.

"The first application to build was turned down very early on. The Council had taken against just in-filling bomb damage." He put his finger on a line of print and read aloud: "They wanted each bomb site developed to its full potential with regard to the future not the past."

"I see. What happened next?"

"Someone in the planning department dreamed up a new road complex for the whole area. Before my time here, of course, but that put a stopper on any development for years and years while they fought it out."

116

"Then what?"

"All quiet until 1960 when an outline application by Mark Reddley (Developers) Ltd., on behalf of G. Hodge, Esquire, was accepted but turned down on detailed plans being submitted."

"That's interesting."

"Things went dormant again after that and then three years ago . . ."

"Yes?"

"The Council shook the dust off their slum clearance plans from before the war. That stirred things up and Reddley put in another design for this G. Hodge." He frowned at the paper in front of him. "Seems as if it was a toss-up who developed."

"The Council or Hodge?"

"That's right. The Council would have powers if they had wanted to use them."

"They were thinking of clearing the area?"

"Looks like it. That side of the road anyway. That would have meant compulsory purchase orders, compensation, and so forth."

"And somebody not the owner doing the developing," observed Sloan thoughtfully.

"True. In the event, though, it didn't come to that."

"No . . ."

"A couple of months ago Reddley submitted another set of detailed plans . . ."

Somewhere at the back of Sloan's mind was someone else's remark about something else changing a couple of months ago, too. He couldn't pin it down and it teased him for a moment or two before he decided it probably wasn't important.

The planning officer was still talking. "These new plans were more conventional from the look of things. Anyway they must have been all right because they got the go-ahead from the Council fairly pronto. It looks as if they went straight ahead quite quickly and started work."

"At long last . . ."

"Planning's like that," said the planner apologetically.

117

As Sloan made his way back to the police station it came to him.

It was the old doctor in the house opposite the bomb site who had died a couple of months ago.

Ten hectic minutes later Detective Inspector Sloan and Detective Constable Crosby joined the small crowd which was clustered round Harold Waite's dead body.

The crowd was of an entirely different composition from the crowd of workmen who had clustered—full of awe—round the other body two days before.

These were police technicians and they were not awed. Cameramen, men with measuring tapes, men with notebooks, police this and police that—the full panoply of unnatural death was being extended to Harold Waite of Bean Street, Luston, number two workshop foreman, sometime sergeant in the West Calleshire Regiment, and late of Lamb Lane, Berebury.

It was the last which had been of deadly significance.

Sloan wasn't in any doubt about that.

"He came over to Berebury to see someone," he said to Detective Constable Crosby.

"We did try to see him first, sir."

"He thought he could do better than we could . . ."

"Twice," said Crosby. "We went back."

"He should have told me," said Sloan bleakly. "He'd have been all right then."

He wasn't all right now.

Sloan waved an arm towards the body. "When did it happen?"

Crosby jerked his shoulder towards Field House. "Dr. Latimer thought something under twelve hours ago but he couldn't swear to it. Said he wasn't an expert on dead bodies."

"He soon will be at this rate," commented Sloan bitterly. He moved over towards the cellar. The police photographer was standing surveying the scene. "Morning, Dyson . . ."

"I must say you don't half have 'em, Inspector," responded the photographer. "Talk about the old and the new . . ."

He nodded briefly, his mind still on Harold Waite. He hadn't been spared after all.

"Ancient and Modern, you could call it," said Dyson, "should you be looking for a caption." Captions weren't a problem for Dyson. His pictures had simple titles like: *View of Deceased as Seen Through Bushes From Roadside and Frontal Aspect of Car Taken Following Collison.*

"I'll remember that," promised Sloan.

"Otherwise we're finished here." The photographer slung some of his camera equipment over his shoulder and beckoned to his assistant. "Unless there's anything else you want taking, Inspector? We've got the usual X-marks-the-spot and wish-you-were-here ones."

"Thank you." Dyson hadn't known the man, of course; hadn't spoken to him as a living human being only yesterday. Sloan shook himself. It couldn't have been only yesterday that he had sat in Harold Waite's front parlour . . .

Dyson waved an arm. "And general-view-of-the-resort. We've done some of them, too. Do I send them to you again?"

"Yes, please."

He nodded to his assistant. "Make a note of that, Williams. All Lamb Lane bodies to the Inspector."

Perhaps Dyson was right to take refuge in flippancy. Sloan didn't blame him.

There was nothing pretty about Dyson's job.

Photographing the aftermath of human folly.

He went a little nearer himself and took a long look at Harold Waite's body. There were two lots of human folly involved here.

Harold Waite's own in playing a lone hand and coming here and the folly of whoever had killed him . . .

Two lots of human folly?

That wasn't right.

There had been three.

Waite's, Waite's killer's, and Sloan's.

Sloan's for being beguiled into thinking that the first murder was an historic affair; not of the present. That there need be no haste about investigating it.

119

He peered down into the narrow grave space which contained Harold Waite and winced. It was of the present all right. He should have . . . he nipped his own train of thought in the bud. A guilt complex wasn't going to get anyone anywhere.

He turned his head abruptly as Dr. Dabbe arrived and stumped onto the site. The pathologist nodded all round—he knew all the police team—and clambered down beside the body.

"This place is turning into a veritable Aceldama, Sloan."

"Beg pardon, Doctor?"

"Don't you know your Bible?" He grunted. "Aceldama. The field of blood, Sloan, to bury strangers in."

"He's not a stranger," said Sloan tonelessly. "He used to live here. The site owner—Gilbert Hodge—identified him. He's gone over to the doctor's house to have a bit of a sit down. Says all this has brought on his ulcer pain."

"Has it?" Dabbe grunted again. Pain was never material to his evidence and he didn't have a lot to do with living patients. "Well, someone hit this chap on the back of the head. Hard."

"We're looking for a weapon now, Doctor."

"And not so long ago as the other one."

"Would about the middle of last night be all right for timing?" The only thing Sloan had paused to do when he got the news about the dead man had been to grab the report on the attack on Dr. Latimer.

The pathologist stared down at the prone figure. "I can't be definite. Not outside like this—but you could be right. Got a witness?"

"I think we could have someone who nearly saw."

Dr. Dabbe snorted. "If you ask me that's all any of them ever do. What you want, I suppose, is dumb evidence. That's what you're after now, isn't it?"

"It's better than the other sort," offered Sloan.

He'd had his fill of spoken evidence in his time.

Eyewitnesses who hadn't actually seen; who had thought they saw; who had jumped (with both eyes closed) to the nearest conclusion; who had unconsciously shut their eyes at the vital moment; who had had their stories rehearsed for them in the nearest public house bar; who saw themselves with a bit part to play and who played it—tripping over themselves to get into the witness box and tripped over as soon as they were in it—be they coached ne'er so well . . .

"Did you get any further with the first body?" The pathologist started on his own routine.

"We haven't made a great deal of progress yet. The most that Miss Tyrell remembered about the night in question," said Sloan, "was that the nightingales wouldn't stop singing."

"Callimachus," said Dr. Dabbe unexpectedly.

Sloan took another look at Harold Waite.

"Not him," said the pathologist impatiently. "Callimachus. That's what he said. A Greek."

"You don't say sir?" Surely they'd had the Greek crack about obols already this week . . .

"Callimachus noticed them too. 'The nightingales sing on—death spares them that spares not anything'."

"Quite." Sloan cleared his throat. "A sort of epitaph for a raid that, sir, wouldn't you say?"

He stood by while the pathologist went about his work. The scene in Lamb Lane was almost exactly the same as it had been on the Monday. The only real sign of change and progress—the great yellow articulated digger—had gone.

"Tomorrow to fresh woods and pastures new," murmured Sloan ironically to himself. He'd liked learning poetry at school. English poetry.

Otherwise what he saw at the site was the same save for the swarming police. The timbers still shored up the adjacent house. The narrow, neglected gardens still ran away from the ruins. Desolation was still the order of the day. What difference there was between then and now lay in the minds of the policemen who were there. Before, their view of the site had merely been the beginning of a new job. Now, they were investigating an old death and a new one.

With undertones of war.

And overtones of murder.

Gilbert Hodge was half-sitting, half-lying on Dr. Latimer's surgery couch. He was holding a measuring glass containing a chalky-looking mixture in one hand. His other hand was covering part of his tummy. His face was about as pallid as the medicine he was taking.

A white-coated Miss Tyrell was standing by. Dr. Latimer was washing his hands. He waved Sloan in with a towel and said, "Would I be right in thinking, Inspector, that I lost my watch in the cause of versimilitude?"

"I think so," said Sloan cautiously. "Local colour."

"It was a good watch."

Sloan cleared his throat. "You could consider yourself lucky you—er—didn't see what hit you."

"Point taken," said Latimer thoughtfully. "It was dirty work at the crossroads all right. I was luckier than that poor devil."

Gilbert Hodge stirred. "You'd called your dogs off, Inspector . . ."

"P.C. Cresswell has other duties today, sir." Actually he'd gone—protesting—to be a traffic light at the Market Place crossroads. Wednesday, the station sergeant had underlined the word heavily, being Market Day. Not so much, he had added gloomily, that they kept the traffic moving, but they did manage to stop it rusting out where it stood. "Not that having the site guarded would have made a lot of difference."

"No." Hodge shrugged. "Someone had it in for old Harold. You don't get hit like that for nothing."

"No, sir." Sloan could guess easily enough why Waite had been killed. "Are you feeling well enough to make a statement about finding him?"

He was but it didn't tell Sloan anything new.

"And you knew him well enough in the old days?"

"We were all part of the same bunch. You think you know people well when you play around with them but you don't."

Sloan agreed with him there. It wasn't play which revealed people.

"And we were all young at the time," said Hodge.

"Yes." The lady in Lamb Lane had been young, too.

"And there was a war on."

122

"Yes."

"You took your fun where you could get it."

"Yes." That certainly applied to the lady in Lamb Lane. Unless he was a Dutchman.

"The old doctor might have been able to help you," said Latimer.

"But he's dead, sir."

Harold Waite would have been able to help too. But he was dead.

Too.

"What about records?" suggested William helpfully, waving his hand towards the banked rows of patients' medical cards. "You must have records, Inspector, just like I've got."

Upon the instant Miss Tyrell surged across the consulting room towards the records, putting herself between them and everyone else. "But these are confidential . . ."

"We've got some records," admitted Sloan, "but not cradle to grave stuff. We haven't got everyone taped."

"Just the sinners," said William. His head was beginning to ache again?

"Yes, sir." Sloan coughed. "I understand it serves us very well."

"If you wait a year or two," said William, "you'll be having my records and I'll be having yours."

"Really?" Sloan got ready to go. Gilbert Hodge hadn't anything useful to tell him. Or if he had, he wasn't going to.

"Someone once said we'll end up by putting ill people in prison and criminals in hospitals."

"It wouldn't surprise me, sir," said Sloan stolidly. "Not nowadays, it wouldn't." He turned to Hodge. "We'll be seeing you again later today, sir, if you don't mind but just for the record you hadn't seen Harold Waite in years . . ."

Hodge nodded. His colour was a little better now but not much. "That's right. Not Harold."

"Not Harold?" quickly.

"Leslie," said Hodge. "I saw him only the other day."

"When?"

"Sometime last week, it would have been." Hodge scratched his head. "Thursday. No, not Thursday. Friday, it was. In the evening."

13

"Say that again, Sloan," commanded the superintendent crossly. "Someone has done what?"

"Killed Harold Waite." Sloan had borrowed Dr. Latimer's telephone in Field House to ring in to the police station. "I want his brother brought over from Kinnisport, please."

"That's bad, Sloan. The chief constable isn't going to like it when he hears."

"No, sir." Neither, of course, would Clara Waite when she did. He'd given the zealous Sergeant Pritchard of Luston that job. Praise be.

"Then there *had* been some monkeying about on that site," snapped Leeyes. No one could have called him slow.

"Someone," said Sloan more succinctly, "altered Mr. Fowkes's pegged out site lines on Friday night so that Rigden and his friends shouldn't dig just where the skeleton was."

He grunted. "Trying to make sure she was never found."

"Yes, sir. And now they've made sure Harold Waite can't tell us who she was either."

"He knew, of course."

"It definitely rang a bell with him," admitted Sloan. "I saw it . . ."

"*The Bells, The Bells*," chanted Leeyes down the telephone.

"Beg pardon, sir?"

"A case where the chap let the murder prey on his mind."

"I don't remember that one, sir."

125

"I told you about it at the time. Quite a good tale, really."

Then it came back to Sloan.

It had been in what had gone down in history at Berebury Police Station as the winter of French Literature.

Each week the morning after the superintendent's Adult Education Class, Sloan had been subjected to a rehash of the lecture. Even now he could remember them. Balzac, Racine, Molière, Maupassant, Lamartine, Proust . . . especially Proust.

Proust was the one the superintendent was said to brood about nowadays when he sat and watched Dick's Dive across the Market Square.

"The murderer there," went on Leeyes, "escaped the gallows but was destroyed by his own conscience."

"I haven't seen any signs of that anywhere yet, sir." Not in those poor grey bones: certainly not in Harold Waite's crushed skull.

Leeyes grunted. "That's the trouble with this case, Sloan. You don't know what you're looking for."

"Not yet, sir." Sloan started to marshal what he did know about who he was looking for.

Or could guess.

Someone who wasn't free to marry at the time of the first murder. Or who didn't want to. A man, of course. Shooting was a man's crime. So was killing mothers-to-be.

Someone who had been around at the time, obviously. And that wasn't the easiest of things to establish after so long. Someone who had been around on Friday night. And last night.

"He'll be middle-aged by now," said Leeyes.

"I suppose he will." And just what did that signify? Hot blood grown cool, perhaps . . . cool and calculating: because if one thing was certain it was that most men became more calculating with the passing years. Sad but true. And there had been plenty of passing years in which to calculate the risks inherent in that buried body. He hesitated. "It's a long time to live with a thing like that, sir. It might have made its mark—like in that chap you've just told me about."

126

"Good for him," declared Leeyes, performing a neat verbal *volte face*.

"I beg your pardon sir?"

"Good for him," repeated the superintendent robustly. "Nietzsche said so."

"Did he, sir?"

Nietzsche.

Sloan recognised that straightaway.

From the winter after French Literature.

Psychology Today.

When the superintendent had upset all the lady cleaners at the police station by following them around and asking them what they did with the contents of their dustbins. It had been by far the most disruptive of all the Adult Edcuation classes that the superintendent had been to.

" 'Build your houses by Vesuvius,' Sloan," said Leeyes. "That's what he used to say to people."

"Really, sir? He didn't mean the volcano, did he?" Sloan was wondering now if Gilbert Hodge's ulcer had a place in this sorry story.

"Of course he did. That's the whole point."

"Why, sir?" Detective Inspector Sloan, that prudent husband, householder, and rose-grower, would have as soon as dreamt of building his house upon sand.

The superintendent said, "He thought people should lead exposed and therefore heightened lives."

"Was he alive in the last war, sir?"

"What's that got to do with it?"

"I just wondered if he'd ever been bombed."

"No, of course not," snapped Leeyes. "He was dead by then."

"I see, sir." He cleared his throat. "Well, whoever—er—did for this young woman had plenty of this sort of life you were talking about. And he's going to have a bit more now. I hope he enjoys it."

"I expect he's got used to it, Sloan. Even that fellow who hung about under that sword hanging by a hair . . ."

"Damocles, sir?"

"Him," said Leeyes grandly. "I expect he learnt to live with it after a bit."

127

Sloan gathered up Crosby and left Field House.

Neither French Literature nor international psychology was going to solve this case.

Just routine. Like talking to the man who lived next door to the bomb site, who might have heard something in the night.

They found him leaning over his garden fence watching the police activity with interest.

"Lived here long?" began Sloan generally. It didn't do to rush the old and retired. They liked to take their time.

"All me life," wheezed the old chap. "Bert Jackson's the name. Anyone'll tell you. Born, bred, and wed here, if that's what you mean by long." He spat expertly over the fence. "And all but dead here too more than once."

"Last night," said Sloan. "Can you tell us anything about last night or about last Friday night . . ."

"Wednesday it was," said Jackson. "Not Friday. The Wednesday. Thought I'd had it that night." He coughed. "They used to say, you know, if you heard it coming it wasn't yours . . ."

"Did they?" This was worse than French Literature or Psychology Today. This was historical reminiscence in the first person singular.

"All my eye," said Jackson vigorously. "Besides— how could they prove it? Tell me that."

"Difficult," agreed Sloan. "Now, about last night . . ."

"Difficult? Impossible! Like with this one on the Wednesday. I 'eard it all right. Started as a whine and sort of rose to a whistle. That's when I took the hint and went down by the doctor's garden wall, over there—see?"

Sloan obediently swivelled round and took a look at the dwarf retaining wall in front of Field House.

"Mind you, mate, I didn't hear the actual bang."

"No?"

"Just felt as if I'd been clobbered all over with a sand bag. No pain. The pavement"—he wheezed—"the pavement seemed to come alive just like one of them things kiddies bounce on at school. What do you call 'em?"

"Trampolines?"

"That's right. One of them. Ground rushed up to meet me." He coughed again. "I rushed down to meet the ground."

"Nasty," said Sloan. Perhaps they could get to the point soon . . .

Bert Jackson sucked in his breath. "So was the next thing, mate. Funniest feeling I've ever felt. Like as if I'd got one them magnets inside me that was pulling me inwards until I was the size of a pinhead."

"You don't say."

Jackson spat over the wall again. "Dr. Tarde, he said afterwards that was the effect of the vacuum from the blast on me lungs."

"Really?"

"That wasn't all."

"No?" Sloan hadn't thought for a single moment that it would be. It wouldn't be often now that the old chap got a chance to tell his bomb story to a new audience.

"No. After that there was this almighty roar."

"Another bomb?"

"No. Same bomb. All the earth what had gone up in the air decided to turn round and come down again."

"And buried you?" suggested Sloan.

"Nearly. Took me a tidy time to shake it off I can tell you. Then I thought I'd gone blind. Everything was black." He spat again with remarkable precision. "Dust and dirt. Couldn't see the moon any more. And as for the smell of exploded powder . . ."

"Quite."

"First thing I did was to look where the bomb fell . . ."

"Naturally." Yesterday Sloan would have been keenly interested. Anything about the bombing which might have led them towards the unknown woman would have been a help. But now they had something more positive still. The late Harold Waite.

Jackson waved a hand at the bomb site. "Nothing much left of these four, I can tell you. And my own house looked as shaky as I felt." He coughed. "I got down to our shelter over there . . ."

Sloan looked. It was still there. At the bottom of the garden. Covered with ivy and full of potatoes.

129

"And my own wife didn't recognise me. Thought the bomb had unhinged her, I did."

"Shock?" sympathetically.

He shook his head. "It was me, guv'nor. I was so dirty she didn't know me . . ." He broke off in a fresh paroxysm of coughing.

"The blast didn't do your chest a lot of good," observed Sloan.

"My chest," cackled the old boy. "That's a laugh, that is. It wasn't Hitler's war that did for my chest, mate."

"Wasn't it? I'm sorry . . ."

"Gas," said Bert Jackson temperately. "In the Salient. Wipers to you. Early in April '15."

Sloan nodded his comprehension. There was a bit of verse—English verse—buzzing around in his mind, pushing its way to the surface. That line about the evil that men do living on after them. . . . The Greeks weren't the only ones who could write about war.

Bert Jackson said, "I pat that wall of the doctor's over there every time I go by."

" 'Thou bleeding piece of earth,' " murmured Sloan under his breath. That described it best of all.

"Beg pardon, sir," said Detective Constable Crosby upon the instant.

Sloan gave him a sour look. Most of the time Crosby looked as if he wasn't paying any attention at all but you only had to . . .

"Shakespeare," he said shortly. "We had to learn it at school."

Crosby subsided. He hadn't.

"*Julius Caesar,*" added Sloan for good measure. "Boys always do *Julius Caesar.*"

At that moment a car drew up in Lamb Lane. A smooth, sleek car, without protuberances. Sloan recognised it from the day before. Two men got out. Garton, the builder, and Reddley, the developer.

"We've just heard about Harold Waite, Inspector . . ." that was Mark Reddley.

"A bad business," contributed Garton.

"As you say, gentlemen," agreed Sloan ponderously.

130

"Knew him well in the old days," said Garton. "One of our crowd then."

"So I believe," said Sloan.

Reddley looked up sharply at that.

"I shall be wanting to know a bit more about the old days." Sloan took out his notebook. "Perhaps, Mr. Garton, you'd tell me what you did in the war?"

"What I did in the war?" Garton had the pale, almost translucent skin that went with ginger hair. Only it wasn't pale any more. It had flared up into an aggressive red. "What is this? A sort of quiz?"

Old Bert Jackson coughed his way into their conversation. "He means did you fight for King and Country, mate."

"You know damn well I didn't." Garton spun round and glared truculently at Jackson. "But I did my bit. We all did."

"What I was getting at, sir," said Sloan patiently, "was whether you were away from Berebury during the war."

"What? Oh, I see. Why didn't you say so? I was here, Inspector. They wouldn't have me in the Services. Diabetic. I tried often enough."

"In that case," said Sloan, "perhaps you can tell me what happened here after the bombing."

Garton frowned. "Alf White and his mob would have given it the once over immediately after. They were the rescue people."

"I bet your old man cleared the rubble," said Mark Reddley.

"I expect he did," agreed Garton. "He never missed a trick."

"Rubble was always wanted," Reddley murmured. "Then and now. Funny that, when you come to think of it."

"I know he used to pay half a crown a yard for the bomb stuff." Garton looked quite wistful. "Half a crown a yard! Do you know what I'm paying now, Inspector?"

"What I would like to know, sir," rejoined Sloan deftly, "is what your father did with the rubble."

Garton scratched the back of his head. "I can guess.

131

The same as he did with every other bit of rubble, aggregate, and everything else he could lay his hands on at the time . . ."

"What was that, sir?"

"Took it down to the airport. Aerodromes they used to call them in those days."

Bert Jackson wheezed over the fence. "Changing everything, they are. Won't leave anything alone these days. Not even names."

"The airport, sir?"

Garton nodded. "We were building runways as fast as we could. Making a bomber station there. Couldn't get enough of anything quickly enough. Dad had the contract. We weren't allowed to do any other sort of building then. Just the odd repair and bomb damage. And you had to have a certificate of essentiality before you could do them."

"The runway . . ." said Sloan.

But Garton wasn't so easily kept to the point.

"Funny how quickly we forget, don't we?" he said. "Especially bad times. You sort of put them out of your mind."

Sloan nodded.

Unless they were really bad like Bert Jackson and his bomb. Then you had a mental picture for keeps as clearly etched on the mind as if it had been truly done by acid eating into copper. Something that took priority in the memory-retaining cells of the brain. Total recall wasn't in it. What you had then was a sort of permanent lithograph ready to run off an impression at the drop of a hat. Or the trigger of someone else's reminiscence.

"The runway," he said again. "When were you building that?"

"Beginning of '42," said Garton. "Scoured the countryside for pebble, aggregate, rubble. Anything we could lay our hands on."

"When did you finish it?"

"April. It went operational in May."

Sloan looked down. "So this ground would have been cleared by then?"

"A bit before that I'd say, if we used the rubble for the foundations."

132

"And all the loose surface stuff would have gone?" Dr. Dabbe had gone now, he could see that, and the late Harold Waite had been taken away.

"And the kitchen stove," said Garton. "If it was moveable we took it."

That might give him another date to work from for the first murder, thought Sloan. On the other hand they had an exact date for Harold Waite's murder and that didn't seem to be helping much. He was aware that Mark Reddley was getting restless.

"Inspector"—Reddley rested a well-shod foot on a couple of bricks—"will your people be long on the site? I know you've got your troubles here but I don't know if you realise quite what a pricey business it is keeping men hanging about like this?"

"Yes," said Sloan rather shortly.

He knew.

And if he hadn't known he would have guessed from that car parked in Lamb Lane. Developing was a profitable game and keeping Mark Reddley waiting would be expensive. He took the initiative.

"I understand, sir, that you undertook to inform the Council that work was about to begin on the site in sufficient time for any archeological excavation to be . . ."

Mark Reddley groaned aloud. "Fowkes and his precious bits and pieces. Yes, Inspector, I told one of my girls to send the Council a post card."

"Which girl, sir?"

Reddley looked up quickly. "I believe I wrote a memo, now I come to think of it. Couldn't say offhand which one of them dealt with it."

"I'd be obliged, sir, if you'd ask because it doesn't seem to have reached Mr. Fowkes yet."

"I'm sorry, Inspector, but I don't think that's my fault. I expect it's stuck on the pipeline somewhere." He grimaced. "My experience is that the only thing that doesn't get stuck at the Town Hall is the rate demand."

"Very possibly, sir, but nevertheless I should like to be told in due course the name of the girl who sent the card."

Reddley raised his eyebrows and said politely, "By all means. Was the historical stuff important then?"

133

"I don't know, sir . . ."

"But I thought they didn't find anything," interposed Garton. "I told Mr. Fowkes they could have all the weekend . . ."

"The fact," said Sloan, "that they didn't find anything might have been because they didn't look in the right place."

"But . . ."

"They didn't look where Mr. Fowkes wanted them to look. If they had"—Sloan paused—"if they had they might have . . ."

"Spotted the lady," said Detective Constable Crosby unconscionably.

14

"Leslie Waite's gone to sea," announced Superintendent Leeyes.

"What?"

"Leslie Waite's gone to sea . . ."

Surely it was Bobby Shafto who had gone to sea, thought Sloan bemusedly to himself, his mind still on the bomb site even though he had now come back to report to the superintendent in his office at the police station. His wife, Margaret, who had a good voice, often sang about Bobby Shafto going to sea. Bonny Bobby Shafto.

"Message just in from Kinnisport Police," said Leeyes laconically. "They say he put out of the harbour about an hour ago."

Sloan nodded, absorbing the information at last.

"At ebb tide, I suppose.'"

"That's right, Sloan. What is this? Another Cain and Abel affair?"

"I'm not sure, sir, yet." He didn't know that he was sure about anything any longer. Only that a girl had died a long time ago and a man last night and that they had both probably died in the same cause—someone else's security.

The superintendent was apparently looking on the bright side. "At least," he growled, "this chap being killed narrows the field."

Was that, thought Sloan, an epitaph for a suspect or did Leeyes think they were playing the game of Ten Little Indians?

"It gives us a list of starters," he agreed drily, sticking to the metaphor. To his way of thinking its metaphors were the only useful part of horse racing; the only thing worth putting on a horse in his philosophy being Lady Godiva. "There's Gilbert Hodge," he said. "I don't know if it's living by Vesuvius that's given him his ulcer or not. And Anthony Garton. He would have known all about both the development and about the archeological digging. And Mark Reddley. All three of them were of an age to be fathers then."

"What about the old chap you've just been talking to?"

"Bert Jackson?" Sloan paused. "He would have known all right but I think we can scrub him. He hasn't got enough wind these days. Not for violence."

"Plenty of that in this case," said Leeyes gruffly. "We're not dealing with kid glove stuff. What about Leslie Waite?"

"Gilbert Hodge said he saw him over here in Berebury on Friday evening," said Sloan uneasily. "But he told me himself he never came this way nowadays."

"Ha . . ."

"Hodge said he saw him," said Sloan. "We've no evidence yet that he was over here."

"You've gone a bit particular all of a sudden, Sloan, haven't you?"

"Garton," persisted Sloan, "mentioned a man called Alf White who was at the bombing—we're looking up his address now."

"That's all in the past, man. What about last night?"

"Last night, sir," forecast Sloan, "will turn out to be a dead loss. I've got Crosby checking but I'm not hopeful. I'm afraid we will find that each of our—er—starters will have gone to bed at his usual time and will have been found in bed in the usual manner in the morning." He flipped over the pages of his notebook. "Luston Police have traced Harold Waite as far as the train which arrived here at half-past seven last evening. We can't find anyone who saw him after he got here."

Leeyes grunted again. "I expect he took good care not to be seen."

When Sloan got back to his own room he found Crosby there.

"The lady in Lamb Lane wasn't the dentist's chairside assistant, sir. She's alive and well and living in London. We just got a message through. She wrote to her mum afterwards and made it up with her, too, though not with the dentist's wife, if you know what I mean."

"I didn't think it would be here," said Sloan. He picked up Dyson's photographs of Harold Waite and started leafing through them. "I think we're dealing with someone who knew better than to write a letter on someone else's behalf."

"Oh?" Crosby didn't sound particularly interested. "And I've got this chap Alf White's address for you."

"Tricky things, letters," said Sloan ruminatively. "A letter gives you something to hold on to . . . something to keep and to go on looking at." The photographs weren't very nice. "You can start to trace a letter and if it's a forgery . . ."

"You smell a rat, sir?" suggested Crosby helpfully.

"Exactly." He looked up. "Do you realise, Crosby, that it would seem no rat was smelt?"

"Yes, sir."

"That's the funniest part of this case."

"Yes, sir."

"Or if," said Sloan profoundly, "a rat was smelt it was more convenient not to say."

"Yes, sir."

"And that doesn't really help."

"No, sir."

Sloan sighed. Crosby wasn't really what you could call a great help either. "And what else have you been doing?"

"Talking to P.C. Brown, sir. Telling me one of his stories he was."

"Was he?" said Sloan savagely. "Well, let me tell you that while you've been. . . "

"It was one of his first blackout jobs in the war, sir. Seems as if he and his mate were out on the beat and they called up to this woman that she'd got a small chink showing in her bedroom. 'You're mistaken, officer,' she calls back, 'It's a Japanese friend'."

Sloan sent him to get the car out.

* * *

Mr. A. White ("Call me Alf, officer, everyone does") of "Mon Repos" Shepherd Street, Berebury, was only too happy to talk to Detective Inspector Sloan about the bombing. Sloan could see the glint of reminiscence in his eye a mile away.

"Yus," he said. "I was in the A.R.P. all right. Air Raid Precautions they called it. If you ask me there was a lot of P. and no A.R. to begin with. But then it really got started and we had the Air Raids all right."

He was a shrimp of a man, bright as button, with an wholly agreeable merriness about him. He knew all about the bodies on the Lamb Lane site. "Having a bit of trouble round there I hear . . ."

"You were there in the beginning," began Sloan generally.

Alf White did not need a second invitation.

"I'll say," he said. "That was a night, the Wednesday."

Sloan nodded mechanically. Listening to Alf White had a place in detection. It came under the "stones and avenues" heading. If you worked for Superintendent Leeyes you left a stone unturned or an avenue unexplored at your peril.

"We didn't know where to go first," said White. "I was attached to Post D round the corner. You know it, I expect, guv'nor. It's the hall where the Brownies meet now . . ."

There was an old saw pit in the village where Sloan had been born which, as hand sawing went out and motorcars came in, had, by much the same token, slipped into use as a garage inspection pit.

" . . . There's a pub down that street . . ."

"The Rose and Crown," agreed Sloan. The Irish labourers might still be there for all he knew, waiting to get at the Lamb Lane site.

"They got that early on." Alf grinned. "There were a fair number of Englishmen with Scotch accents about that night, I can tell you. Then after a bit the fire up at Corton's got going. It looked like five sunsets all rolled into one." He shook his head. "We didn't need no torches while Corton's was burning."

"No . . ."

"First chap we found was in the road right outside the Post. He was the greengrocer from the shop opposite the pub. We got him into the ambulance and he came round with a drop of something nice." He grinned again. "And I don't mean blitz broth."

"Blitz broth?"

"Soup." Alf drew breath. "A proper comic was that greengrocer. Do you know he was back the next morning with 'I have no pane, dear mother, now,' chalked on the boards where his windows had been."

"That's the spirit," said Sloan.

"We came by the church first," said Alf, mentally retracing his steps with less difficulty than many a yesterday's witness. "That hadn't half caught it. The old vicar was standing in the churchyard looking at what was left. Charlie Hibbert—he was a bit of a wag, was Charlie—he called out, 'I see we got a Leaning Tower now, too, Vicar,' but the old chap didn't take no notice. Do you know what he was doing?"

"No," said Sloan. He knew what he himself should be doing. And it wasn't listening to Alf White. It was sitting down and thinking hard about who it was who had known all about an unborn baby, a bullet, and a body.

"He was standing," said Alf White, "by one of the graves looking at the church and chanting something. It seemed so queer but proper church-like at the same time. I've never forgotten it. 'O ye fire and heat, Bless ye the Lord.' "

Detective Inspector Sloan, erstwhile choirboy, coughed and said, "It's from the Benedicite."

"You don't say?" said Alf. "Well, Charlie said we'd better make sure the old boy hadn't gone round the twist so I went up to him. 'Come, lovely Death,' he was saying as I got near to him. 'Walt Whitman, Alf,' he said, but I hadn't time to stop really. He didn't last long after that—too many miles on the clock when the war started."

"Lamb Lane," said Sloan unwillingly, turning his mind from the vivid word picture sketched by the little man.

"A shambles," said Alf promptly. "They said that

139

they thought there was someone still in number two and so we started the digging and tapping routine. We never got no response and then someone turned up with a message that everyone had been accounted for after all. That would have been about two o'clock in the morning."

"Tell me,' said Sloan, "if, after that, someone had wanted to bury a woman in the cellar, could they have got down there?"

Alf shook his head decisively. "No, guv'nor. Definitely not. Not unless he was a ruddy mole or something. All those houses were struck all of a heap, so to speak. You couldn't have got under anything until they were cleared."

"What about after that?" The pathologist had said after that.

"After? Oh, it would have been quite easy after the top stuff had gone. You could have got down there and dug away to your heart's content." He grinned. "It wouldn't even have upset the neighbours seeing as how there weren't any neighbours left to upset."

"No one would notice a little bit of digging, of course," murmured Sloan aloud. It had just come to him who would in all probability have known about the unborn baby—if not about the bullet and the body. Dr. Tarde. Unborn babies were a doctor's business.

"Notice?" Alf White grinned again. "There was so much digging and rubble shifting and people scrabbling about that I reckon you could have buried what you liked. Come to that, you could have parked what you liked in some of the ruins, too. The only risk was the kids finding it. Charlie—now he kept his black market . . ." Alf White suddenly recollected to whom he was speaking and his voice faded away.

"You've been a great help," said Sloan, diplomatically deflecting the conversation. "What about your own house?"

"I did think it had had it when I got back and saw the street. You know, I didn't care very much at the time. Funny, really, when you think how cross I get if the paper boy kicks the fence."

Sloan turned to go.

"It wasn't all bad, guv'nor. Wouldn't want you to think that. I met the missus fire-watching." He poked Sloan in the ribs. "You couldn't think of a better place for courting. Not in a month of Sundays."

"You must have had some bad days all the same," said Sloan.

"I only got really worried the once," confided the little man. "That was at the Whitsuntide Bank Holiday the year before."

"What happened then?" asked Sloan curiously.

"It was the Council Offices . . ."

"The Council Offices?"

"That's right," said Alf seriously. "They stayed open all the Bank Holiday weekend. I knew things must have been pretty bad for that—but as I used to say to the wife—everything has an end and a piece of string has two." He brightened. "We A.R.P. people still have a Reunion, Inspector, each year. If you was wanting to talk to any of the others—they haven't forgotten anything you know . . ."

Sloan went back to his office. He hadn't been there long when Crosby knocked on the door.

"Can I bring in those marriage certificates now, sir?"

"You can bring in the dancing girls," growled Sloan, "if you think it's going to do any good."

"From Somerset House, sir. Just arrived by special delivery. Notes on those marriages you asked me to get." He brought them in, together with two cups of canteen tea. "Reinforcements for the inner man, too, sir."

Sloan sighed. What he could have done with was reinforcements of quite another sort. Like a detective sergeant with a trained mind—ready, willing and able to help him sort out this impossible tangle of the old and the new. An officer with—what was it fashionable to call it these days? An officer with a low threshold of suspicion. At the very least a man with a mind above his stomach, who thought history began yesterday.

He picked up the first of the pile of records that Crosby had brought in. "I see Gilbert Arthur Hodge married Annie Briggs."

"Did he?" said Crosby indifferently.

"And she," said Sloan, "from the look of their respective addresses was the girl next door."

"Not very enterprising," agreed Crosby, reaching for the second one on the pile. "Listen to this, sir. Mark Reddley married Constance Blake-Mobberley, daughter of Godfrey Blake-Mobberley, F.R.I.B.A., Consultant Architect . . ."

"Well done that boy." Sloan took a drink of tea. It was very welcome. He'd forgotten when he was next due to eat. "Who's next?"

Crosby pointed. "Number three. Garton."

"Oh, yes. Here we are. Anthony Garton, son of Anthony Garton . . ."

"Garton and Garton," said Crosby, "like their board says."

"Anthony Garton," said Sloan repressively, "married Winifred Grimston of Cullingoak."

"Change the name and not the letter," chanted Crosby, "change for worse and not for better."

"I beg your pardon, Constable?"

"It's true, sir. You look at that woman I went to see this morning . . . the Gretna Green one."

"Murgatroyd?" The Lamb Lane lady hadn't been her either.

"She's called Marshall now. It didn't do her any good."

Sloan picked up the next paper. They were investigating a murder—two murders—not playing word games. "Miss Tyrell . . ."

"Miss Tyrell?"

"The General Register Office," said Sloan austerely, "report that they are unable to trace any record of any marriage by Millicent Amy Tyrell."

There was a hoot of merriment from Crosby. "You didn't think they would, did you, sir? Not with a face like that . . ."

"There's no art, Crosby, to find the mind's construction in the face."

"Pardon, sir?"

"Nothing," he said wearily. "It's a quotation. When I

was a constable our instructor always used to begin his lectures with that."

"Oh."

"Lesson One it was, on people. To stop us judging them by their appearance."

"Oh."

"Lesson Two," said Sloan grimly, "was not to rationalise the obvious." There had been nothing in those lectures, though, about what you did when there wasn't any obvious. "And don't forget that even Miss Tyrell was young once."

"Not her," retorted Crosby. "I don't believe it."

Crosby wasn't unsympathetic. It was one of the things which was making this case so difficult.

Just how did you begin to imagine what a middle-aged person had been like in the days of their youth? It was like looking at a flower in September and wondering about June. Sere, stringy leaves and dried-up seed pods didn't tell you anything about fresh green leaves and fine flowers.

Somehow, though, he still couldn't imagine Gilbert Hodge as a dashing young man—but both Garton and Reddley could have been good lookers once. He knew Leslie Waite had been because Miss Tyrell had told him so. Harold Waite—before he turned stocky—had probably looked quite well. Better than he did now, anyway.

Especially in uniform.

He said as much to Crosby.

"I expect," said that worthy inarticulately, "that they were like themselves now but less so, if you know what I mean, sir."

Even that was no great help when Sloan came to think about Dr. Tarde. He had never known what he had looked like. Older than the others anyway. And his wife had died young. In 1935, Somerset House said.

Sloan picked up the next paper.

"Harold Waite married Clara Hitchens, daughter of Herbert Hitchens, draper, of Shepherd Street, Berebury."

"Biggest mistake he ever made, I'll bet," pronounced

143

Crosby, who was himself still seeking the perfect wife and who hadn't yet settled for someone he loved instead.

It wasn't Harold Waite's biggest mistake. He'd made a bigger mistake than that last night when he left Luston and came over to Berebury on his own. Sloan winced inwardly. He shouldn't have done that. He should have stayed in Luston.

"Fancy being spared for twenty-five years of Clara Hitchens," said Crosby.

"And Leslie Waite," went on Sloan, taking up the last paper of all off the desk, "married Freda Cowell of . . ." he stiffened suddenly. "Crosby, what was the name of that lady we saw Leslie Waite with last night . . ."

"That was no lady, sir," responded Crosby immediately, "that was his . . ."

"Crosby!"

"Sorry, sir. Doreen, sir."

"That," said Sloan softly, "was what I thought it was, too."

15

"Get me Somerset House again," commanded Sloan swiftly, "and get on to County Headquarters at Calleford as quickly as you can and ask them to send a police launch out after that boat of Leslie Waite's at Kinnisport."

"Yes, sir."

"Do we know what it's called?"

Crosby nodded. *"The Saucy Nancy."*

Sloan hadn't time to wonder if that was significant or not before the Town Hall came through on the telephone in the person of a Mr. Mallinson.

"I understand you were asking about the bombing, Inspector . . ."

"Yes, please," said Sloan. It seemed like a hundred years ago at least when he had made his enquiry. It must have been yesterday.

"We don't have a Civil Defence Department any more, Inspector."

"I hope," said Sloan politely, "that means you don't have any bombing either."

The voice at the other end of the line said, "If you've only got four minutes . . ."

"Quite," said Sloan. He didn't know himself what defences there were against attack now that ramparts were out. England had run through them all in time—ditches, drawbridges, boiling oil, barbed wire, anti-aircraft guns. Nobody had invented an aerial portcullis.

Mr. Mallinson said, "I don't know what'll happen next time, I'm sure."

Neither did Sloan. As far as he could see four minutes would be long enough for Police Constable Light-

145

ning Brown to put his helmet on—but that was about all.

"I expect," said Mallinson unenthusiastically, "that it'll all fall on us first . . ."

Sloan supposed it would, too, politics being what they were these days. Or had it stopped being "politics" and become "failed diplomacy" by the time the bombs began to drop?

"Just like it did last time," the man went on.

"Quite," said Sloan. But there was a difference between now and last time. Fallout wasn't just a barrack square phrase any more. He didn't know what prophylactics there were against bombing nowadays. Perhaps there weren't any. Perhaps that was why there were those who rallied to the cry of "Make love not war." Perhaps they weren't so far off beam after all. Odd if the Dick's Dive crew were right and everyone else was wrong . . .

Sloan shook himself. He must pull himself together.

He told Mallinson what he was enquiring about.

"Bombing comes under the Ministry of Housing and Local Government," said the man from the Town Hall, "but don't ask me why!"

"It's the recovery of someone from a bombed building."

"Ah, that's different. That's not the Ministry of Housing and Local Government."

"No?"

"That's the Secretary of State and the Home Office."

"Even if they're dead?" asked Sloan mildly.

"I expect," sighed Mallinson, "that's the Ministry of Health though I can't be sure offhand. It's all covered by Statutory Instruments, you know."

So, thought Sloan silently, was most police procedure, but that did not alter the fact that it was how the individual member of the authority behaved at the point of contact with the individual member of the public that really mattered in the long run.

He coughed. "I was wondering about your records. You must have records."

Mallinson gave a hollow laugh. "It wouldn't be a Town Hall, now, would it, Inspector, without records."

146

"No, but . . ."

"You've only got to sneeze . . ." Mallinson cleared his throat. "About the other . . ."

"Yes?"

"We confirm that no notification of the proposal to commence building work pursuant to the Town and Country Planning Acts of 1947 and various subsequent building bylaws had been received by the Building and Planning Department."

"Ah . . ."

Mallinson said, "I expect we'll forgive them this time as they obviously haven't got very far."

"What would you have done with the notification if you'd got it?" said Sloan.

"Sent a copy round to Mr. Fowkes at the Museum first then one of our Building Inspectors would have gone along later to look at their foundations. To make sure they complied with the regulations."

"And to see they weren't too near Vesuvius," murmured Sloan softly.

"Vesuvius, Inspector?"

"Nothing," said Sloan hastily, and rang off.

Constable Crosby came back just then with some notes about Dr. Tarde. Sloan had asked for those, too, in an absent moment. Aeons of aeons ago. He leafed through them rapidly without interest.

It had been in June that Dr. Tarde had died.

Sloan read about the inquest.

Unhappily.

There had been an open verdict.

Nothing to show why deceased had taken his own life.

If he had.

There was certainly nothing to show why he should have done.

There were no financial worries. (Confirmed by his executors.)

He wasn't ill. (Confirmed by post-mortem.)

He didn't think he was ill. (Confirmed by Miss Tyrell.)

147

He had been found hanging from a beam in his garage, a chair kicked to one side.

There had been no note.

The coroner didn't like suicides without notes and said so.

The last person to see him alive had been . . . Sloan turned over a sheet . . . Mark Reddley.

Mark Reddley deposed that he had called to collect a prescription for his wife and that then the doctor had been sitting at his desk, writing.

The coroner recalled the police officer who had searched for a note.

There had been no note on the desk or anywhere else.

It had been Mrs. Milligan's night off.

The body had been found by a policeman on the beat later that night.

The coroner had enquired how that had come about.

The doctor's car, it seemed, had been standing in the road without any lights on. The man on the beat had gone in to look for the doctor to tell him this, found the house unlocked but empty and flashed his torch round the garage . . .

Sloan put the papers down. Dr. Tarde was in the clear anyway. He hadn't been around last night to kill Harold Waite.

"The only chap," he said, "in the ordinary course of events with a good reason for having known about the pregnancy . . ."

"And he goes and hangs himself," concluded Crosby gloomily.

"Say that again . . ."

"He goes and hangs himself."

"The only person," said Sloan, bringing one hand down on top of the other with a healthy smack, "in the ordinary course of events with a good reason for knowing about the pregnancy—being a doctor—and he goes and kills himself just before the site is about to be cleared. That means . . ." He spun round and looked at Crosby. "Suppose that Dr. Tarde didn't commit suicide, Crosby. Just suppose that for one minute . . ."

"Yes, sir."

"Well?"

Crosby scratched his chin. "If he was killed, too, sir, I'd say that that would mean that if this body was dug up he would have guessed who . . ."

"Might have been able to guess," modified Sloan automatically. Qualified statements were better in the long run than the categoric variety.

"Might have been able to guess," said Crosby agreeably. "Like Harold Waite."

"And look what happened to him. Perhaps, Crosby, we've started from the wrong end . . ."

"By the way," said Sloan hastily, "there was something else I wanted to ask you, Doctor. Tell me, suppose you wanted to fake a hanging, how would you go about it?"

"I'd garotte whoever it was," responded Dabbe promptly. "From behind. Preferably while he's bending down to do up his shoelace . . ."

"Or picking up something you've just dropped accidentally on purpose," suggested Sloan.

"That's the idea. Put your knee in the small of his back and heave. Remember to jerk your rope or what-have-you upwards as well as backwards. Then you'll get your marks in the right place. That way it's pretty difficult for the pathologist to tell . . . Sloan, are you trying to suggest that . . ."

"Thank you, Doctor, you've been a great help."

"There's one other thing, Sloan."

"Doctor?"

"The chair. Better men than you have forgotten the chair."

Sloan rang off.

The chair hadn't been forgotten.

The superintendent was still at his desk staring out of his window across the Market Square. He was only half-sitting down—being poised the while to rise on the instant anything happened outside Dick's Dive opposite. It was a physical attitude which had been dubbed throughout the police station as "The Watch Committee Watching."

"Well, Sloan?"

"Leslie Waite is living with a woman called Doreen, sir."

"What about it?"

"We've just found out that he married a girl called Freda Cowell during the war."

"What happened to her?" enquired the superintendent alertly. "Is she your body?"

"I don't know, sir. We're trying to find out now. I've asked the Register Office at Somerset House to do a special search for me as quickly as possible."

"No news from Kinnisport Police?"

"Not yet, sir. They haven't had a lot of time . . ."

Leeyes grunted.

"This Doreen that he's living with," ventured Sloan tentatively, "could be a second wife. Freda Cowell could have divorced him or died ordinarily."

"And my name could be George Washington," snapped the superintendent smartly.

"Just as likely," agreed Sloan as gravely as he could.

Now why had the superintendent chosen George Washington for his simile? According to those lectures on Psychology Today, potted versions of which had reached Sloan each week, the choice of George Washington must mean something.

"But it isn't," said Leeyes unnecessarily.

"No, sir." Had it been, wondered Sloan, what was called a Freudian slip? When you unconsciously revealed that which you—consciously—wished to hide? Perhaps the superintendent had a secret yearning to be thought of as a man who could not tell a lie.

Because, if so . . .

"This is the one who was cut out of his father's will, isn't it, Sloan?"

"Yes, sir. Old Ernest Waite left the house—or rather what was left of it—to Harold only."

"Have you found out why?"

"Not yet, sir." Perhaps Freda Cowell could tell him. If she was alive. If he could find her.

"There must be a reason. It wasn't entailed, was it? It's not a Stately Home or anything like that."

"No, sir. Just an ordinary house."

150

"Primogeniture," rumbled Leeyes, "doesn't usually count for much in families like the Waites."

"No, sir." Sloan cleared his throat. "There's just one thing that's worrying me about Leslie Waite . . ."

"Well?"

"He doesn't come into any of those arguments about the rebuilding. Neither does Harold Waite, come to that. He definitely sold the site in 1946—we checked with the Land Registry—and hasn't figured since."

"Until yesterday," said Leeyes smartly.

Sloan hadn't needed reminding. "He only had to tell me, sir . . . I'd have stopped him coming over if I'd known."

"A criminologist," pronounced Leeyes sagaciously, "is always someone who is wise after the vent."

Was that meant to be a crumb of comfort? Sloan didn't know. He pressed on: "I think, sir, we may be nearer a time for the first murder."

"Oh?"

"Towards the end of the winter after the bombing. Say about February or March of 1942. That's when the loose rubble was cleared. It wouldn't have been before then."

Leeyes said acidly, "Now I suppose all we want is someone who was a first-class rifle shot thirty years ago and bob's your uncle."

"They were all good shots," pointed out Sloan. "The Waites and Gilbert Hodge were in the Services and Reddley and Garton were in the Home Guard."

"And it's too late to ask them what they were doing on the night in question." The superintendent's view of detection was a very simplified one. Sloan had noticed this before.

"Even if we knew the night . . ."

Leeyes drummed his fingers on the desk. "This planning business then that the Waites didn't come in to . . ."

"A proper tangle of delay, restriction, and heaven only knows what, sir, until a couple of months ago when everything suddenly resolved itself all at once."

It was like offering a fresh scent to a bloodhound. The superintendent's head came up with a jerk. "Why?"

"It was the Council, sir. About three years ago they said they were going to go ahead with some old slum clearance plans . . ."

"About time, too," growled Leeyes.

"Well, it seems they'd just about got round to thinking about it properly last May or June when Mark Reddley and Associates slapped in some acceptable plans and got them passed pretty quickly."

"So it was a toss-up who developed?"

"For a little while, anyway. Then Mark Reddley, acting on behalf of Hodge, got the go-ahead and Garton's men got cracking quite smartly."

"Funny, that," mused Leeyes.

"Yes, sir." Sloan admitted that. It was odd that everything should suddenly fall into place after a quarter of a century of delay and debate.

But the superintendent wasn't listening any more. An abstracted look had stolen over his face. He was staring out of the window at Dick's Dive opposite. A van had just pulled up outside it, and a number of remarkably undifferentiated young men and women were tumbling out of the back and going inside the cafe.

"Dear Sir or Madam, as the case may be," muttered Leeyes sardonically. "Look at that, Sloan."

Sloan obediently looked at the van.

There was no part of it not painted with flowers.

"Flower power," said Leeyes scornfully. "What do you make of that? Look at them! Where shall we be, Sloan, when they're our only army?"

"I couldn't say, sir, I'm sure." Very probably, he thought, in the same situation as they would be if they weren't. He made for the door. "I daresay we'll have to have a new Geneva Convention." Perhaps the only real hope was that there wouldn't be an army. What was it that someone was postulating? That these unaggressive youngsters were Nature's response to the manufacture of wholesale weapons, chain reactions, total destruction. Nature always bent herself in the direction of the survival of the species . . .

* * *

Constable Crosby was in Sloan's office when he got back.

With more tea.

And some news from Somerset House.

In the circumstances, read the message sheet, they had made a priority job of Inspector Sloan's request for information.

"Nice of them," said Sloan. With murder cases time was usually of the essence and, even if it wasn't, the press hounds baying on the police heels always made it seem as if it was.

"Item," said Crosby, reading aloud, "there is no record in the General Register Office of any death being registered in the name of any Freda Waite née Cowell from natural or any other causes."

Sloan got out his notebook.

"Item," said Crosby, still holding the paper, "there is no record of any marriage having taken place between Leslie Waite and a woman called Doreen . . ."

"Ah . . ." Sloan drank his tea and considered this.

"Item," continued Crosby, "there was a son born to the aforementioned Leslie and Freda Waite . . ."

"The devil there was!" Perhaps they were getting somewhere after all.

"Name of Brian Ernest."

"That didn't make any difference," said Sloan elliptically.

"Er—what didn't, sir?"

"Calling him after his grandfather. Everything still went to brother Harold." Sloan put down his cup. "Get out an all stations message about Freda and Brian Waite. Anyone knowing their whereabouts . . ."

"Will do . . ."

"If they don't find Freda Waite," Sloan said, thinking ahead, "it still doesn't account for the fact that she wasn't recorded anywhere as missing."

"No, sir," Crosby nodded. "Then it'll be like Mrs. Sloan said at breakfast this morning, won't it?"

"What do you mean?" growled Sloan. He wasn't having his wife's name bandied about at the police station by young detective constables.

"Everyone must have thought she was somewhere else. Like Mrs. Sloan said," he went on awkwardly, "they didn't think she was missing because they thought they knew where she was. Only . . ." his voice trailed off lamely, "she wasn't."

16

"I just don't understand," said a bewildered Miss Tyrell. "Are you trying to tell me that Dr. Tarde shot that girl?"

"No, miss. He didn't shoot her. Or kill Harold Waite either, come to that." Sloan had found Miss Tyrell still at Field House, still in her official-looking white coat. He had sent Crosby out into the back streets of Berebury to see what he could find out about a woman called Freda Waite, née Cowell. Dr. William Latimer had gone out again on his afternoon round.

"Well, then, what . . ."

"Miss, if there were any young lady hereabouts who was having a baby, who would be most likely to know about it?"

She smiled a little. "I think I would, Inspector."

"And who else?"

"The doctor, of course, but he's new still. It'll take a little time before . . ."

"Naturally. But before. When the old doctor was alive?"

"Ah, that was different." Her brow cleared. "He'd have known . . ."

"Yes, miss. I think he would. It's something I should have thought about before."

Her head came up sharply. "He wouldn't have killed that girl."

"No."

"He was a doctor, Inspector. He was dedicated to saving life, not wasting it."

"Yes, miss, of course." Sloan didn't argue: though a first-class medical training hadn't stopped those well-

155

remembered doctors Harley Crippen, Buck Ruxton, William Palmer—Palmer, the poisoner—Lamson, Cream, Smethurst, and Petiot from doing murder in their day. It would seem the medical training had, if anything, helped. "But would he have known about the baby?"

Miss Tyrell adjusted her glasses and favoured him with a thoroughly intelligent stare. "I see what you're getting at, Inspector."

He thought she would. Why did people decry sensible women so? They were certainly a pleasure for a police officer to deal with.

"What," said Miss Tyrell slowly, picking her words with obvious care, "you are inferring, I take it, is that if Dr. Tarde had known about the pregnancy then, he might have been able—had he been alive now—to have put a name to that unfortunate girl whom they found opposite?"

"Just so, miss." He was in no doubt about in which sense Miss Tyrell was using the word "unfortunate."

In the same sense as his mother would have used it.

"Then," she said flatly, "it's lucky for someone that he's not."

"Very lucky," agreed Sloan at once.

Her head came up with a jerk at that. "I never believed myself that it was suicide."

"I am beginning to feel," said Sloan cautiously, "that I could make out a case for its not having been. There was no note, for instance."

There was in this case, he had already noted, a distinct absence of the written word altogether. It would seem that there was someone abroad too clever to play about with forgery.

"You mean," said Miss Tyrell, "if it wasn't suicide it was someone actually wanting him out of the way?"

"It's a possibility that we're bound to consider."

"That would mean, Inspector"—Miss Tyrell took out a spotless white handkerchief and began to polish the lens of her glasses—"that Dr. Tarde would have known who she was."

"Yes."

"And that very few other people did."

"You're very quick."

She acknowledged this with a faint bow of her head. "One of them being Harold Waite?"

"I'm very much afraid so."

Miss Tyrell put away her handkerchief and replaced her glasses firmly on the centre of her nose. "It may be a strange thing to say, Inspector, but it would be a great comfort to me to know that it wasn't suicide."

"Yes, miss, I can understand that. It was in June, wasn't it?" It had been about then, too, that the plans for the redevelopment of the Lamb Lane site, which had been on the files for upwards of twenty-five years, had suddenly taken a great leap forward.

"That's right." She sighed. "The house seemed full of death then. Mrs. Cardington—she was the doctor's old housekeeper—she had only just died."

"What about relatives, miss?" The old doctor's connection with the case was still obscure but it was there. He was beginning to be sure about that. Sloan wanted to know all he could now about Dr. Tarde. "His wife died years ago, I believe."

She nodded matter-of-factly. "Before the war, even. There was no family—just a second cousin of his and a niece on his wife's side—and she lost touch during the war . . ." Her voice trailed away as she caught sight of the expression on Sloan's face.

"Do you mind saying that again, miss, please . . ."

"She lost touch with the doctor during the war," faltered Miss Tyrell. "His wife's sister's girl. Margot. She left here one night and didn't come back. The doctor never heard from her again."

"Didn't he?" and Sloan quietly. "Didn't he indeed?"

"For my money," Sloan informed Crosby, "she's Margot Elinor Poulton, Dr. Tarde's wife's niece."

"She's not Freda Waite, anyway, sir," returned Crosby briskly, slapping his notebook down on Sloan's desk. "I've just been talking to her. She's living in Park Street calling herself a widow. Under the name of Cowell."

"Margot Poulton was last seen alive," said Sloan meaningly, "early in April 1942." Miss Tyrell hadn't been sure about the date, hadn't remembered the girl particularly well. Margot Poulton had only been in the habit of visiting her uncle at Field House. She didn't live there. Miss Tyrell hadn't seen her at all on her last visit of all to Dr. Tarde. "You can guess why that was, Crosby, can't you?"

"Yes, sir. Didn't want Miss Tyrell to know about the baby."

"I'll bet that's why she came back to Berebury, though," said Sloan.

"To have a word with the boy friend," suggested Crosby brightly, "and to ask him what he was going to do about it."

"I expect," said Sloan with heavy irony, "That she was all for a shotgun marriage."

"And someone didn't like the idea of marrying her?"

"Or by then they liked the idea of marrying someone else better." Sloan hesitated. "She doesn't seem to have been everyone's cup of tea."

It had been marvellous the way in which the genteel Miss Tyrell had conveyed this information to him. A couple of nice nuances and a few unspoken sentences had told Sloan that on the whole the doctor must have been quite relieved when she had apparently taken herself off and not come back.

"So," said Crosby intelligently, "whoever killed her guessed Uncle Henry wasn't going to be too keen on finding her. Especially as he thinks she'll have an illegitimate baby in tow."

"She doesn't sound as if she would have added to his professional standing locally," agreed Sloan. "I don't think he would have looked too hard for her."

"It was like Mrs. Sloan said then," persisted Crosby with unusual doggedness. "Everyone thought she was somewhere else."

"London," said Sloan. "That's where she'd come from. That's where they thought she'd gone to. They certainly didn't think for one moment that she was only across the road."

"No."

"That doesn't mean to say, of course," said Sloan, developing his argument as he went along, "that if a pregnant young woman of the right age and the right vintage had happened to have been disinterred there that they wouldn't have put two and two together and made four."

"That's what Harold Waite did, I suppose, sir."

"Harold Waite knew her, too. Miss Tyrell said she had an idea he was something of an old flame."

"Neat to bury her under his house then," said Crosby.

"Very. If she's found he's the first person who is going to be asked about her."

"And the old doctor would have put two and two together like you said, sir."

"Bound to. If he'd been alive to do it." Sloan coughed. "There was someone else who would have done, too. If she'd been alive."

Crosby's head came up enquiringly.

"A Mrs. Cardington. The old doctor's housekeeper. She died of a heart attack in May."

"Natural?"

"Natural. But I think it was trigger to everything that's happened since. It was only when Mrs. Cardington died that someone began to feel safe enough to make a move. She remembered Margot Poulton very well, you see."

Dr. Latimer kept his visits brief that afternoon. He'd already seen the really ill patients in the morning and his head was hurting again. He was also getting distinctly irritated by the continuing kind enquiries about the bandage. He drove back to Field House therefore as quickly as he decently could

Miss Tyrell was still there at her desk though she should normally have gone home ages ago.

She greeted him with shining eyes.

"Dr. Latimer—about Dr. Tarde—such good news. That police inspector—you know the one I mean—so nice and respectful—quite respectable too, really, when you come to think about it—he's been back again and do you know—he says he thinks Dr. Tarde didn't commit suicide after all. Isn't that a comfort?"

"Was it an accident then?" suggested Latimer, bewil-

159

dered as much by Miss Tyrell's sudden talkativeness as by what she said. "Surely the question of accident was sorted out a long time ago?"

"No. Not accident. He thinks he was murdered."

"By whom?"

Her hands fell helplessly into her lap. "There now. I quite forgot to ask him."

Superintendent Leeyes jerked his shoulder in the general direction of the telephone on his desk. "There's a message in for you, Sloan, from Kinnisport Police. They've located Leslie Waite in *The Saucy Nancy*. They say they've taken him in tow and they're heading back to harbour now."

"It isn't Leslie Waite, sir."

"They say he didn't seem too put out. Not a worrier, I suppose. That's what I said, Sloan, remember. It'll be someone who could live with himself and his memories."

"It isn't Leslie Waite, sir."

"What do you mean, man?" barked Leeyes. "What about this Freda Cowell he married?"

"Alive and well and living in Park Street, St. Luke's."

"What's that?" The superintendent swivelled round in his chair and glared at Sloan.

"Crosby's just been talking to her, sir. And Leslie Waite still sees her each month."

"Maintenance?" divined Leeyes swiftly.

"I expect so, sir."

"So that's why his father cut him out of his will. I thought there'd be a reason for that. For playing about with this Doreen woman . . ."

"Or someone similar." There would always be women willing to play Leslie Waite's sort of games.

"But she doesn't know about Freda?"

"Probably not," conceded Sloan. "I expect that's why he lied about his having come over here on Friday evening."

"Well, Sloan . . ." Leeyes looked him up and down and then said balefully, "are you going to tell me what you propose to do or are you just going to do it?"

In the event Dr. William Latimer didn't get his longed-for peace and quiet that afternoon after all. He had barely had his first cup of tea when Mrs. Milligan came rushing through with the news that there had been a bad accident outside Mr. Reddley's office and would he go at once.

He did.

He could tell that something serious had happened from the way in which people were crowded round in the street—but crowded at a distance from something that was lying on the pavement. It was as if they were equally reluctant to move either nearer or farther away.

Somewhere he could hear a girl crying.

"It was the drawing office window," she said between sobs. "He said the sash was stuck. He got up on the sill and said he'd fix it and then . . ." She started crying again.

Someone led her away.

Dr. Latimer took a quick look at what was lying on the pavement and saw for himself why it was everyone else was keeping their distance. It wasn't pretty. It was Mark Reddley.

On the fringe of the crowd he recognised Detective Inspector Sloan and Detective Constable Crosby but they made no move to speak to him. In the distance he could hear the clangour of the approaching ambulance siren.

He straightened up, his own headache forgotten. He supposed the only useful thing he could do now would be to go round and see Mrs. Reddley.

The superintendent didn't seem to have moved since Sloan last spoke to him. He was still sitting at his desk overlooking the Market Square.

"I suppose Reddley saw you coming?"

"Yes, sir. I think so. From his window."

"You weren't actually waving the warrant, I hope."

"No, sir." They hadn't flaunted it from the street but then they hadn't attempted to hide their purpose either. "I think he knew we were coming for him."

161

Leeyes grunted. "And now you're going to tell me you knew it was him all along?"

"No, sir. But I did know roughly when and how and why the girl was killed and so when . . ."

" 'I keep six honest serving men'," quoted the superintendent jovially. "Do you know that one, Sloan?"

"Yes, sir." Sloan sighed. He knew it all too well. Someone had once—in a misguided moment—taught Superintendent Leeyes what they had called the policemen's poem. Rudyard Kipling's. *The Serving Men*. Sloan hoped they had lived to regret it.

" 'They taught me all I knew'," sang on Leeyes.

"Yes, sir," responded Sloan politely. It was not for him to say that the policeman's lot was not a happy one.

" 'Their names are What and Why and When . . .' "

"Quite so, sir." Sloan himself preferred a more neutral police approach: like "And what appears to be the trouble, madam?" or even—at a pinch—Constable Crosby's "Now then, now then, you can't do that there here."

" 'And How and Where and Who'," finished the superintendent triumphantly.

"As far as the Who is concerned, sir . . ." There was only ever one way to take the superintendent and that was literally.

"Well?"

"There was only one person who fitted in every particular and that was Mark Reddley. He married an architect's daughter for a start. That must have given his career a leg up. And he did all the different designs for the various development projects on the Lamb Lane site over the years. Garton and Hodge didn't do that. I checked. And their marriages weren't important to their careers either."

"Marriage is always important to a career, Sloan. You should know that."

"Reddley," said Sloan, ignoring this cynical aphorism, "must have been able to tell in advance that his designs would be rejected when he wanted them to be and also accepted when he thought the danger was past."

162

"Last June . . ."

"One danger was past, sir. Mrs. Cardington had died. But a fresh danger had arisen. That was that official planning had reached such a pitch that the Council were going to develop if Reddley didn't."

"So the old doctor had to die, too."

"I'm afraid it looks like it."

"Anything else?"

"It was Mark Reddley and Associates who should have given proper notification of intended digging for foundations to the Council so that Mr. Fowkes at the Museum—among other people—should know about it. And he didn't."

"Didn't want the archeologist grubbing about," agreed Leeyes sagely.

"Certainly not, sir. And he didn't want the Council doing the designs either. He wanted to do the layout himself."

"I can quite see that. To reduce the chances of the skeleton being found in the first place."

"Yes, sir." Sloan frowned. "I should have guessed earlier about that. Gilbert Hodge kept saying he couldn't understand why Reddley designed the new building like he had done. He also told me Reddley wanted some symbolic statuary there . . ."

"Ha! Now at those Psychology classes I went to, Sloan . . ."

"Reddley was too clever to buy the land himself," went on Sloan hastily, "but he took steps to keep in with Hodge. If anything did happen to be found suspicion was bound to fall on the Waite brothers first and then Gilbert Hodge."

"Only Harold Waite thought he was cleverer."

"Or, perhaps, he just wanted to do a little checking on the quiet first."

"He was unlucky," said Leeyes.

"So was Reddley," said Sloan. "I reckon he had two bits of bad luck actually. The man putting the marker in just happened to strike that spot. That was something he couldn't foresee."

"And the other?"

"The bullet staying in the body, sir. Its lodging in the

163

spine like that was pure chance. And without the bullet we'd never have known it was murder . ."

The superintendent wasn't listening any more. He was staring out of his window as if mesmerized.

"Look, Sloan. At Dick's Dive. Over there. That hair. It's halfway down the chap's back. And waved . . ."

Sloan gathered up his notes and made for the door. Mark Reddley's hair had been cut to regulation length, his appearance routinely masculine and his clothing rigidly conventional. And he had killed—quite ruthlessly—the three people who stood between him and his personal ambition. Perhaps the hair didn't matter after all . . .

Detective Inspector Sloan hadn't been back in his own room very long before Detective Constable Crosby came in.

"Message just through from Mr. Esmond Fowkes, sir. The Museum man."

"Well?"

"He's been working on the Lamb Lane site, sir. Looking for those Saxon remains."

"Has he indeed?"

"Seems as if he's found them, sir. Some bones. Late Saxon. Wants to know what to do with them . . ."

Sloan told him exactly what he could do with them.

ABOUT THE AUTHOR

CATHERINE AIRD had never tried her hand at writing suspense stories before publishing *The Religious Body*—a novel which immediately established her as one of the genre's most talented writers. *A Late Phoenix, The Stately Home Murder, His Burial Too, Some Die Eloquent, Henrietta Who?* and *A Most Contagious Game* have subsequently enhanced her reputation. Her ancestry is Scottish, but she now lives in a village in East Kent, near Canterbury, where she serves as an aid to her father, a doctor, and takes an interest in local affairs.

WHODUNIT?

Bantam did! By bringing you these masterful tales of murder, suspense and mystery!

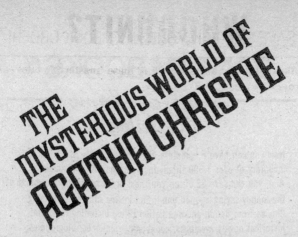

THE MYSTERIOUS WORLD OF AGATHA CHRISTIE

Acknowledged as the world's most popular mystery writer of all time, Dame Agatha Christie's books have thrilled millions of readers for generations. With her care and attention to characters, the intriguing situations and the breathtaking final deduction, it's no wonder that Agatha Christie is the world's best-selling mystery writer.

☐	20435	**SLEEPING MURDER**	$2.75
☐	20986	**A HOLIDAY FOR MURDER**	$2.50
☐	14851	**POIROT INVESTIGATES**	$2.50
☐	20155	**THE SECRET ADVERSARY**	$2.50
☐	14847	**DEATH ON THE NILE**	$2.50
☐	23557	**THE MYSTERIOUS AFFAIR AT STYLES**	$2.75
☐	22626	**THE POSTERN OF FATE**	$2.50
☐	14039	**THE SEVEN DIALS MYSTERY**	$2.50